THE EGGPLANT EMPEROR FROM ANOTHER DIMENSION IN MY BROTHER'S CLOSET

MALSMAN LAKE 1

ADAM J. MANGUM

ROCKET CROSSING

ISBN: 978-1-945359-22-4

For Lena, Clare, Jane, Hannah and Benjamin

ALSO BY ADAM J. MANGUM

Malsman Lake

The Dream Queen and the Fate of Malsman Lake

The Empire of the Peaks

Assassins & Rebels

Peak Crosser

Wayward Flight

Crumbling Empire

Light of Moons

The Sycorax Series

Caliban's World

Seeds and Masters

Claribel and Caliban

CHAPTER 1

FINDING a house that had completely disappeared should
have been, by far, the weirdest thing that had ever
happened in Samantha Stadler's life. But she lived in
Malsman Lake, Minnesota, and despite an entire home
missing from where it had been the day before, it seemed
more normal than weird. In Malsman Lake, weird was just
part of life, so much so that people seemed to ignore even
the truly bizarre.

A year before, the Sjostrom family, who lived two doors
down from the Stadlers, had awoken to find a Komodo
dragon in their backyard instead of their black lab Viking.
So, it being Malsman Lake, they had just called the big
lizard "Viking" and acted as if nothing had happened. Mr.
Sjostrom even took the Komodo dragon hunting, though
from what their son Henry said, the lizard was a terrible
tracker and ate the only pheasants he found.

Two years ago, when Samantha was in third grade, one of their teachers, Mrs. Wilson, had come to school with horns. Not big horns like a ram, but little horns that were barely visible through her bangs. That first day, Samantha and her classmates screamed, and one kid even ran to Principal Gardner. When the principal arrived, she said Mrs. Wilson had always had horns and that it wasn't nice of us to make fun of someone for being different. No one even mentioned anything two weeks later when the horns disappeared.

Now, on the Saturday at the tail end of spring break, Samantha stood before a house that should have been there. She had been riding her bike out of town toward the lake when she noticed that the Schumacher house wasn't where it was supposed to be. The entire two-story house was gone, like it had been lifted off into space. No debris, no sign of a storm or fire or anything that would explain a house disappearing.

Whatever strange force had taken the Schumacher house had left one remnant behind: the basement. The below-ground level remained untouched, as if someone had built and furnished a basement but forgot to finish the house on top. Mr. Schumacher's purple-decorated man cave was intact, as was the playroom and guest room. The stairs out of the basement were there, but they didn't lead to anything.

"What did I miss?"

Samantha turned to find her best friend Rahul Patil pulling up on his bike. Rahul was nearly as thin as she was, with a tuft of unruly black hair standing on his head. He wore a faded Minnesota Twins t-shirt and red athletic shorts.

"The Schumacher's house," Samantha said dryly.

"Holy crap!" Rahul's eyes went as wide as she'd ever seen them go. "I hope the family is ok. Where's the fire department or the sheriff? I mean, a disappearing house should bring somebody here."

"I overheard Dylan say they were going on vacation to Florida," Samantha replied. Dylan was the Schumacher's oldest child, and he was in the fifth grade at Malsman Elementary School, same as Samantha and Rahul. "I think he said they'd be back on Sunday."

Rahul raised his eyebrows. "Listening pretty closely to what Dylan Schumacher is saying, hey Sammie?"

Sammie (only adults called her Samantha) shifted her weight to her left leg and leaned close to Rahul. "Oh? And where did Chloe Weathers go on vacation, Rahul? Didn't you tell me she went to Canada to visit her grandparents?"

He wrinkled his nose. "That's totally different. She told that to the whole class!"

"I was there, Rahul; I don't remember."

He huffed and looked back at the house. "Forget Dylan and Chloe. I'm not sure what's weirder: that an entire house is gone, or that no one seems to have noticed."

Rahul set his bike down and approached the foundation. The Schumacher house was on the edge of town on several acres off a back road. It was surrounded by trees, but it was March in Minnesota and there was still snow in the shade and no leaves on the trees. So anyone passing by should have noticed a missing house through the dead trees, just as Sammie had.

Sammie set her bike down and followed Rahul closer to the topless basement. "Maybe no one has driven by."

"Maybe." Rahul stood with his Converse sneakers right at the edge of the basement concrete. "Creepy. It looks like we're looking down on an enclosure in a human zoo, well, except there's nobody in it."

Sammie kept back a few steps. "I'm not sure we should be getting too close."

"Close? Are you kidding me? I'm going to climb down."

Sammie stepped closer and grabbed his arm. "Something took this entire house. This isn't like Mrs. Crawford's cabbages sprouting strawberries. This could be dangerous."

"You're the Queen of Weird," Rahul replied, pulling his arm away. "You love all this stuff. Heck, every time something weird happens, it's like Christmas for you. And you don't want to check it out?"

It was true; Sammie loved all the strange. Her closet had become her List of Mysteries: pictures, stories and thoughts about all the weird things happening in Malsman Lake. But all those oddities had seemed harmless. A

Komodo dragon was cooler than a black lab. Cynthia Rudding had looked better with purple hair than she had with blonde.

But this one felt different. Dylan's house was missing, and his family would come home tomorrow to find everything gone. Something about this turned Sammie's stomach into a bunch of little knots.

"Something bad is happening, Rahul. I can feel it."

He laughed. "Come on. You read too many books. There's not always a bad guy and a plot. Weird stuff just happens. All those Sideralis Academy books are making you see a mystery in everything. You're too obsessed with that stuff."

She couldn't deny she loved Sideralis Academy. It was a series of books, movies, and video games about a girl and her two friends at Sideralis Academy, the training ground for the Star Wizard Guild. Heck, she was wearing a Star Wizard Guild shirt.

"Not as obsessed as you are with the Twins," she shot back, narrowing her eyes. "Weren't you the one who thought you saw Joe Mauer at Cub Foods?"

"It was Mauer!"

"Why would a guy who makes like a billion dollars and pitches for the Twins--"

"He's not a pitcher, Sammie. He was the catcher, and then played first base and designated hitter before he retired. And he was shopping at Cub." He sighed. "I'm sorry about poking you about Sideralis. But it's a missing house, Sammie! Let's check it out. Please?"

The knots in Sammie's stomach hadn't gone anywhere, but her curiosity blossomed. She'd ran toward weird her entire life, loved the mysterious stuff that happened in Malsman Lake. Could she pass up the chance?

"Ok. Let's do it."

A crooked smile grew on Rahul's face, and he bounced with anticipation.

Rahul went first, lying down and then pushing backward until he fell into Mr. Schumacher's Viking-themed man cave. His slide was awkward, and he fell onto his backside when he landed. Sammie crouched down, pivoted on her left hand, and then fell into the basement, landing in a squat.

Sammie had never been in the Schumacher house. Dylan and his family had moved to Malsman Lake four years before in the middle of first grade. Dylan kept to himself, laughed at the right times, and was good at sports. Rahul and Sammie were not as popular because they never stopped talking, they always seemed to laugh at the wrong times, and neither of them were good at sports, despite Rahul's love of baseball and football.

The Schumacher basement seemed completely normal, except for the fact that the sun was shining into it. The first room was the Minnesota Viking room: purple paint on the walls, purple leather recliners, and a purple-clad bobblehead collection on the mantle over the gas fireplace. The bobbleheads all nodded slightly with the breeze, which made the lonely basement even creepier.

"They have the 2011 Fran Tarkenton!" Rahul said with amazement, moving toward the bobbleheads.

"What are you talking about?" Sammie wasn't sure why she was whispering, but it seemed appropriate.

Rahul didn't whisper. Ever. "Fran Tarkenton!? The greatest QB in Vikings history?" He pointed at the bobble-head in the center of the collection, like seeing that small plastic face would help Sammie learn something she'd never known. "They gave this out at the 2011 home game against the Bears, but there was a problem, and only five thousand were available instead of twenty thousand. Super rare."

"How can you possibly know that and not be sure if you changed your socks?"

He looked down at his socks, invisible under his jeans. "I'm pretty sure these are from yesterday."

Sammie rolled her eyes. "Let's focus on finding some-thing weird and then get out of here. I don't think a rare bobbleman counts." The bad feeling she'd felt since arriving wouldn't let go, and she wanted to leave before something worse happened.

They continued on into the playroom, a large princess castle in the middle. Dylan had two younger sisters, and the room seemed to favor them more than it did a ten-year-old boy. There was a dress-up area, a castle filled with Barbie-sized princess dolls, and a play kitchen with bright pink dishes.

But in the far corner, she saw something she recognized: a poster of the first movie in the Sideralis Academy series, Danger in the Stars. For a moment, Sammie's bad feeling disappeared as she approached the small section of the room. Below the poster was a small bookcase filled with Sideralis books and figures, and a Star Wizard Guild robe. Displayed most prominently was a 10-inch-tall figurine of Andromeda Rodriguez, the main character of all the books and movies. Dylan Schumacher was a Sideralis fan!

"I thought we weren't geeking out over stuff." Rahul stood next to her, his arms folded and his eyes narrow.

"Dylan Schumacher is a Sideralis fan," she said, repeating her thought from moments before.

"Yeah, well, better to keep that particular geekiness hidden. But seriously, Sammie, turn around and look at the basement. Do you see what I see?"

Sammie reluctantly turned away from Dylan's Sideralis collection and looked back at the basement. At first, she saw nothing out of the ordinary. She saw the playroom and the Viking-themed room beyond it through double doors. But then she noticed what Rahul was talking about—a green mist hanging like a fog in both rooms. It glowed and pulsed to a rhythm she couldn't hear.

"What is that green stuff?" she said, her bad feeling back and stronger than ever.

"So you see it too?" Rahul whispered this time, at least his loud version of a whisper. His feet shifted in the thick carpet. "It's like fog, but there's a breeze and it's not moving." The bobbleheads nodded in the next room, agreeing with Rahul.

Sammie had seen this green mist before. Three years ago with her family, they'd hiked to the top of Lutheran Hill and looked down on the valley. A similar green mist had hung over the clear water of Malsman Lake. She'd asked her parents, and neither of them had seen it. She'd wondered often since then if she'd ever really seen it, or if it had been her ever-active imagination. But here it was again, hanging in the Schumacher basement the day their house disappeared into nothing.

The mist wasn't really like fog, though. It didn't move, but hovered there like a moment frozen in time. And it pulsed with green light; Sammie didn't remember noticing the pulsing three years before.

"I really think we should get out of here," Sammie said, barely able to get the words to come out.

"Yeah," Rahul replied, a rare one-word response.

Just then, the sound of feet shuffling on the gravel driveway broke the green-tinged silence. Sammie and Rahul looked at each other, eyes wide.

"We should hide," he choked out.

She nodded, but her feet were frozen in place as the sound grew closer to the basement, until it stopped seemingly right above them. Then a head appeared above them, deeply shadowed in the morning sun.

The head spoke. "What beneath God's yellow sun are you two doing here?"

It wasn't just a head, but it was connected to a body. And it wasn't just any head and body; it was the town sheriff, Vera Masters.

Sammie and Rahul looked back at each other, the green mist no longer their biggest problem.

CHAPTER 2

WITH SHERIFF MASTERS'S HELP, Sammie and Rahul climbed from the basement. They stood next to her car, and she faced them, her arms folded, her face in a scowl.

Vera Masters was a tall woman, built like she would have been as comfortable on a football field as she was as a police officer. She wore her brown hair short with some blonde highlights. Even when she was shopping at Walmart, she wore her uniform. Sammie had wondered if the sheriff even slept in it, gun and all.

Sheriff Masters led the three-person Malsman Lake police force. Her two deputies were locals, but Sheriff Masters came from Chicago, and because Sammie hadn't met many folks from Chicago, she imagined the entire city was filled with people like Sheriff Masters: tough, stern, and lacking any sense of humor. Chicago did not seem like a nice place.

"I should arrest you both for trespassing. And did either of you consider that it might be dangerous to climb into the basement of a house where the top floors are missing?"

"One of us considered it," Sammie said, folding her arms.

"Well, next time, listen to that person." Sheriff Masters shook her head. "I know you two love all the weird stuff in this town, but this isn't a picket fence changing color overnight. I have no idea what happened to this house, and I don't want to add hurt kids to today's list of bad news."

Sheriff Masters was the only adult Sammie had ever heard even acknowledge the weird stuff that happened in Malsman Lake.

"I was riding up to the lake on my bike and noticed the house missing," Sammie said. "I'm sorry, Sheriff, but I couldn't resist."

The sheriff's face softened. "I know, Samantha. But this one could be dangerous." She looked back at the house. "And I imagine the Schumachers aren't going to be happy about this. How on earth do I even explain this on a phone call?"

"What brought you out this way, Sheriff?" Rahul asked.

"The Schumachers asked me to keep an eye on their house, and so I was coming out to check on it. Didn't expect to find it missing." She shook her head and looked away. "Some days I think I should move back to Chicago where things aren't so strange." She looked back at the kids. "Now go home and don't come back here, okay?"

Both kids nodded in agreement.

"Should we keep it a secret?" Rahul asked, his eyes eager.

"Nah," the sheriff said. "Secrets don't keep in a town this small. And anyways, folks will forget about this one in a week; in any other town, this would be the biggest thing to happen in years." She shook her head and started circling the now-gone house.

Sammie and Rahul biked back toward Sammie's house, going as fast as they could. They always raced each other, no matter the distance. Sammie nearly always won, because she was daring on her bike while Rahul was more cautious. She beat Rahul this time with ease.

"I hit a weird patch of dirt," he said, one of his favorite excuses for losing. "Slowed me down."

Sammie just smiled.

The Stadler house sat near the center of town, only a few blocks from Main Street. They put their bikes on the lawn, still dead from winter. It was spring break, but the snow had only melted off the lawn a few days before. More snow would probably come before spring really arrived.

Sammie's house was nearly one hundred years old and her dad spent much of his free time, and his money, making it look nice. He'd painted the outside a bright white with dark blue trim and shutters. Rahul had been disappointed at the trim color choice; he'd wanted it to be Viking purple.

Once inside, Sammie shouted, "Rahul and I will be upstairs in my room."

"Hello, Rahul," Sammie's dad Randy called from the other room. "Try not to trip over all her clothes on the floor."

"I'm used to the chaos, Mr. Stadler," Rahul answered back.

"You don't have to encourage him," Sammie said, elbowing Rahul in the ribs.

"You do leave a lot of crap on the floor."

Sammie rolled her eyes, but she knew it was true. Rahul's room looked like it was professionally cleaned every day. How could she compete with that?

As soon as they reached the top of the stairs, Sammie's little brother Colin appeared from his room, his head of bright blonde hair in a mess. Colin was four and Sammie's only sibling. He was also annoying.

"Hey Rahul. Want to come play Superman with me?" Colin wore his biggest grin.

"Maybe in a little bit," Rahul answered. Rahul had two older siblings who were in college, so he thought Colin was adorable. That was only because he didn't have to live with him.

Colin put on his biggest pouty face, the face that usually got Sammie's parents to start shoving him full of ice cream.

He looked up suddenly, the fake pout replaced by bright excitement. "Can I play with you guys? Can I? Please?"

"Go bug Dad," Sammie said, ushering Rahul into her room and shutting the door behind them. Colin wailed outside.

"You're so mean to him," Rahul said.

"It's the Saturday of spring break," Sammie complained. "I've spent twenty-four-seven with him all week. He's driving me nuts." Other families went places for spring break, but not the Stadlers. Mom had to work at the bank finalizing loans for farmers, and her dad used the week to get projects done on their ancient house, which left Sammie to entertain Colin most of the time.

"Anyway, forget Colin," she added. "We've got something new for the List of Mysteries."

Sammie stepped over yesterday's clothes. It really wasn't that messy. There were only three small piles of clothes and plenty of empty space. And she always put the underwear away, because otherwise Rahul got really weirded out.

She pulled open the closet door to reveal the List of Mysteries. Sammie had removed all the clothes and old toys from her closet the previous summer to make room for their collection of weird stuff. There were dozens of documented strange events she and Rahul had organized by geography. Most of the weird stuff happened in town or near the lake. Once you got out into the county, things seemed to get normal. Sammie had once met a girl from Rushford, which was only a few miles away, at a Bible camp. The girl had said that the weirdest thing that happened in Rushford was a cow born with a fifth leg. She'd hardly believed Sammie's stories of the strange stuff in Malsman Lake.

Sammie and Rahul had pictures, newspaper clippings, printouts of internet stories, and some handwritten documents they'd put together themselves. On the back of the door was where lake stories were, and Sammie saw a perfect spot to put their account of the disappearing Schumacher house.

"We didn't take any pictures!" Rahul exclaimed. "I had my phone on me and everything." He pulled out his smart phone and waved it around. "How dumb was that? The house could be back tomorrow."

Rahul had a smart phone, but Sammie didn't. She didn't think it was a money thing; they took a vacation every October to someplace nice, and her parents bought her a nice bike for her last birthday. Sammie thought it was a "kids shouldn't have a smart phone" thing, though her parents hadn't ever said why and Sammie had never asked. Most of the kids her age had a phone.

"We'll just have to draw it and write down what we saw."

Rahul stepped closer to the closet door, his eyes on the

lake. "You've seen the green mist before? Why didn't I remember that?"

He pointed to a small index card taped to the door. She'd written down the story of seeing it from Lutheran Hill. It hadn't seemed like a big deal when she'd written it down; she'd pretty much forgotten it herself. It hardly ranked high on the List of Mysteries.

"I thought it was nothing, just fog. But now. . ."

"I think I've seen it before too," Rahul said, crossing his arms. "Remember when my parents and I found that pig who barked like a dog? I thought I saw some green then, but it was gone so fast that I thought I'd imagined it."

Sammie moved the clutter on her desk to reveal a small box of crayons. She pulled out forest green and stepped into the closet. She found the small piece of notebook paper that held Rahul's account of the barking pig and marked the corner with a big green 'x.' Then she did the same on the corner of her Lutheran Hill index card. As she made the second 'x', a headline from an old newspaper story caught her eye: "Saint Mark Lutheran Church: The Anniversary of the Church's Demise."

Lutheran Hill was named for an old church that had been on the hill a long time ago. She pulled the story down from the closet and spread it out on her desk; Rahul crowded in behind her.

Saint Mark Lutheran Church: The Anniversary of the Church's Destruction

Tuesday marks 60 years since the Saint Mark Lutheran Church was destroyed on what is now known as Lutheran Hill. The church had been one of the landmarks in Wabasha County and a pillar in the Malsman Lake community.

The destruction of the church has always been a bit of a mystery. A storm demolished the building, leaving only the basement behind and the pieces so scattered that very little of the church was recovered. Though residents could not remember hearing a tornado, the destruction indicated that it must have been a powerful storm. At the time, residents did recall seeing a strange fog roll off Malsman Lake that morning, with one resident describing it as "pea soup green."

Commemoration services will be held at Lutheran Hill on Saturday morning at 10 a.m., sponsored by King of Kings Lutheran Church and the Malsman Historical Society. Light refreshments will be served.

Sammie looked over at Rahul. "Green fog? No debris? Whatever happened to the Schumacher house happened to that church!"

"What does it mean?" he asked. "Strange things don't usually repeat." He looked into the closet. "I mean, it's almost always just one time. There's only one Komodo dragon who used to be a dog, only one teacher who came to school with horns, and only one cat has walked on a ceiling."

Sammie looked back at the news story. It was dated August 10, 1971, so the incident on Lutheran Hill had been in 1911. That was more than a hundred years ago. It was the oldest evidence they had of Malsman Lake mysteries.

A sharp knock on the door made them both jump. Her dad stepped into the room.

"Rahul, are you ignoring texts from your parents?" He wore a fake stern expression.

Rahul pulled his phone from his pocket. "Oh man, mom texted me like eight times."

"She just called me. She'd like you to head home for lunch and homework. She said Sammie could come over to your house this afternoon." Her dad's eyes combed Sammie's floor. "Hey, you can see some floor! Nice job!"

"I'm rolling my eyeballs in case you can't see," came Sammie's reply.

Her dad laughed at his own joke and left, leaving the door open.

Rahul typed a quick reply to his mom and stuffed the phone back into his jeans. "This is big, Sammie. I mean, what if something is really happening? What if this is more than just the normal weird?"

Sammie stepped back and examined the List of Mysteries. Why had she become so obsessed with all this? Almost everyone in Malsman Lake ignored the strange. But not Sammie, and not Rahul. Maybe they'd been paying attention for a reason.

"We need to do more research," she said. "We need to

find out if there were other disappearing buildings or green fog."

"That sounds a lot like homework," Rahul groaned. "Speaking of which, I can't believe Ms. Dillwater assigned homework over spring break. What kind of monster gives homework over spring break?"

Ms. Dillwater was the new fifth grade teacher at their school. She was young, which usually meant a nice teacher, but not in the case of Ms. Dillwater. She never joked around and always addressed the class with a voice that said, "I know you're all going to do something awful today, so I'm going to treat you that way ahead of time." When Mrs. Fredericks had retired, they had all rejoiced; she was prone to falling asleep during class and she smelled strongly of prunes. But somehow, Ms. Dillwater was even worse.

"That's why I finished it the first day," Sammie said, her eyes not leaving the List of Mysteries.

"Well, I'm going to go eat some lunch and finish mine. I'll text your dad later. Maybe we can meet at the library instead of my house?"

Sammie nodded. "Do you think it could happen again?"

Rahul shrugged. "It was more than one hundred years between the two disappearing buildings. I don't know if we'll live long enough to see another one."

As Rahul dashed from the room, Sammie stepped into the closet to pick out the other big weirds they needed to dig deeper into.

Sammie walked into school the next Monday, spring break gone too fast. Her trip with Rahul to the library on Saturday had been useless; they hadn't been able to find any more references to green mist or fog, and the librarian had chased them out when Rahul asked her about potential references to disappearing buildings or a pulsing green mist. His overly-loud whisper always annoyed librarians, even when his requests weren't bizarre.

Despite her complaints about boredom over spring break and having to watch Colin more than she watched TV, school seemed like a poor alternative. Despite some boredom and too much little brother, she had hung out with Rahul three times and read Sideralis book 4, Killer Comets, for the twelfth time. She liked learning, but she didn't like dealing with the other kids.

Malsman Elementary was small, and she'd been going to school with basically the same kids for six years. Two things were quite clear about Sammie's standing with the kids in her class. First, she didn't share many interests with them. The boys were into sports, hunting, fishing and tractors. Sammie didn't like any of that. And the girls were into music, social media and binging on shows. Sammie liked classical music, didn't have a social media account, and she rarely watched TV except for the animated Sideralis Academy show.

Second, was her mother. Shannon Stadler was a vice president of Malsman Farm Bank, and her primary business was working with local farmers. During good times, that meant everyone was very nice to Sammie's family because her mom gave out money. But during bad times (and times weren't great), Sammie's mom said no a lot and, even worse, the bank sometimes took land or equipment when farmers couldn't pay. That did not help Sammie's popularity.

And if she was honest, there was a third thing: her complete obsession with Sideralis Academy. Sure, almost every kid in school had seen the movies or read some of the books. But Sammie was obsessed, and apparently the only obsessions allowed in Malsman Lake were killing deer and wearing leggings. Maybe if Sammie went hunting in fashionable leggings she'd get more friends.

Sammie arrived at her cubby and, as she hung up her coat, she saw Dylan Schumacher reach his space. Like Sammie, Dylan had blonde hair, though his was short. He wore a blue t-shirt and some shorts, which was weird for a cold rainy day like today. But of course he was. His family had returned from vacation in Florida yesterday to find their house and all their stuff gone. He was probably wearing clothes he'd taken on vacation.

Dylan Schumacher loved Sideralis Academy. Sammie could tell from his display in the basement that he loved it. The collection was amazing, and some of the stuff was recent. He was a fan, just like Sammie was a fan.

As he unloaded his lunch, Sammie thought about talking to him. Today was probably not a very good day for him, worse than the usual "after spring break" blues. His house was gone. He could probably use a friend. And they could always talk about Sideralis Academy now that she knew he was into it. Heck, Sammie could ask him which domus he belonged to. There were three domus at Sideralis Academy: Aurora, Nebula and Umbra, and each incoming student was placed in one of the three. Through the website SideralisAcademy.com, Sammie had been chose for Nebula, the same domus as Andromeda Rodriguez, the main character of the series.

Sammie shook her head and looked away, getting out her notebook. How would she approach a kid she rarely spoke to? Hi, Dylan, I found out that you love Sideralis Academy like me because Rahul and I snuck into the basement of your missing house. Which domus are you in? She blushed just thinking about how stupid she would sound.

The day started as it always did, with Ms. Dillwater lecturing. For someone who'd chosen to teach children, she didn't seem to like kids. This lecture was about how all the class probably wasted their spring break, filling their heads with lame movies and shows and not learning anything or helping anyone. Ms. Dillwater made sure everyone knew that she'd spent her spring break helping flood victims down south.

Ms. Dillwater was a mystery like everything else in

Malsman Lake. When they'd heard the name the summer before, Rahul had drawn what he thought a Ms. Dillwater should look like: old with a big wart on her nose and glasses as big as her head. Only the last part turned out to be at all accurate. She was young, so young that on the second day of class, one of the parents had thought she was a high school student. She was shorter than the tallest boy in class, Chris Shatner. She had black hair to her shoulders, wore glasses with frames so big that some kids had started calling her Ms. Bugwater. And she was pretty. Some of the boys had seemed to notice that, which Sammie found so annoying. They were in fifth grade and she was an adult. Gross!

"So let's try to get your corrupted heads back into learning," Ms. Dillwater said, finishing her lecture. "First up today is science. Let's see, we have eighteen kids today, and we're going to be doing quite a bit of group work, so let's split into six groups of three."

The class buzzed as chairs scooted and voices raised to find their groups of three. Rahul came over and sat next to Sammie, and it quickly became clear that no one would be joining them, despite Ms. Dillwater's clear instructions.

As the class quieted and the groups clustered, Ms. Dillwater folded her arms and shook her head. "This should have been simple, but I see four groups of three, one group of four, and one group of two. Could someone join Sammie and Rahul please? If not, I will re-make the groups myself."

Rahul looked down, his face dejected. Rahul felt as

apart from the class as she did. Though he was into the right sports (baseball and football), he stood out for several reasons. The most obvious was his skin. He was one of two kids in their class of twenty-one students who wasn't white. Rahul's parents had come from India to go to college in the United States and then stayed here in Minnesota. His family ate food most considered bizarre, they didn't celebrate Christmas, and his father had never hunted deer or pheasant. And it didn't help Rahul at all that he'd befriended Sammie.

"I'll join their group, Ms. Dillwater." Dylan stepped away from three other boys he'd been teamed with.

Their teacher smiled and spread her arms. "See, class? It's not that hard to be decent human beings. Thank you, Dylan."

Dylan walked slowly over to them, plopping down in a seat next to Rahul.

"Sorry about your house, dude," Rahul blurted out.

Dylan shrugged as Sammie elbowed Rahul in the arm. "Well, it wasn't the best end to a vacation," Dylan said.

"Did you have fun in Florida?" Sammie asked.

He shrugged again. "We mostly did princess stuff for my sisters. So, not my favorite. The beach was cool."

Their conversation ended as Ms. Dillwater called for attention and gave them instructions on their in-class assignment. She pulled out a bag of potatoes and explained that they were going to make batteries.

"I'd rather make potato chips," called out Chris Shatner, who was so much taller than everyone else that his desk could barely contain him.

"Potato chips are terrible," Ms. Dillwater said, surprising no one with her dislike for the snack, "and irrelevant. Now, who knows why potatoes make good batteries?"

Ms. Dillwater spent the next several minutes explaining the activity and handing out potatoes, nails, wire, clips, steel wool and some cheap little clocks. Despite all that had been going on, despite Dylan's disappearing house, Sammie found herself drawn to making the battery work.

Unfortunately, Rahul was not focused at all on the potato batteries. As soon as Ms. Dillwater said they could start, he peppered Dylan with questions.

"Where are you living?"

"In the hotel on the edge of town, at least until the insurance company and my dad can figure it out. Not sure if we're covered for a disappearing house."

"What do you think happened?"

This question earned another shrug. "I don't know. Mom says it must have been a freak tornado, and the sheriff agrees that it was probably some storm. But dad thinks that's ridiculous. He says there would be something left of the house. He's determined to figure it out."

Sammie had been trying not to listen, trying to focus on inserting nails into the potatoes and connecting them with copper wires. But Dylan's last comment pulled her eyes and mind to him. His dad wanted to figure it out? In her entire life, she'd never heard of an adult who had wanted to solve one of the strange Malsman Lake mysteries. Usually it was the opposite; usually adults said it was nothing and moved on.

"What does your dad think happened?" Sammie asked.

Dylan fiddled with one of the alligator clips, opening and shutting it. "You'll think he's nuts."

"We're considered the two crazy kids," Rahul responded. "So nuts is totally normal to us."

The other boy responded with a short laugh. "Do you two always act like this?"

"Not when we're sleeping," Rahul shot back. "Though, to be fair, I don't watch myself sleeping."

Dylan laughed again, which probably meant Rahul would try to crack jokes for the rest of class.

"Dad thinks it's connected to all the weird stuff that happens in town," Dylan said, his voice low. "Ever since we moved here, my dad has been weirded out by this place. Mom says every place has its quirks, but Dad says those quirks don't include lizard dogs and cotton candy that floats like balloons."

Rahul smiled. "That cotton candy was weird. Remember that kid who ate a ton, and then he could dunk a basketball for the next hour?"

Dylan's face lit up, his gloom mostly gone. "I know, right? I mean, I remember looking up and seeing some cotton candy float away, and pointing it out to my mom, and she said that it must have been made with helium or something. That doesn't even make sense."

Dylan's animated voice had carried and earned several turned heads, including a severe glance from Ms. Dillwater. The three of them looked down at their potatoes and continued their work on the experiment.

As Rahul connected one wire to the clock, Dylan added in a whisper, "I mean, Malsman Lake is weird. So many strange things happen. But it's usually little stuff, not big stuff like a house."

"It's happened before," Sammie added, looking over to make sure Ms. Dillwater wasn't paying close attention to them. Luckily, she was focused on Gavin Hunter, who'd tried to connect the wire to his braces. "Lutheran Hill. That old church disappeared the same way."

Dylan let go of the potato and looked at her. "I thought it got knocked down by a storm."

"That's the story," Sammie continued, "but we just looked at an old news story that said there was no debris, just like your house. And. . ."

Sammie stopped, looking away as if she were checking on Ms. Dillwater again. Should she tell him about the green mist? Could she do that without telling him that she and Rahul had been in his basement and seen the same thing?

"And the story talked about a green fog," Rahul added.

"Did you guys see anything like that?" Rahul winked at Sammie.

"Seriously?" Dylan said, struggling to keep his voice low. "Dad said he thought he saw something like that when he went there with the sheriff and the fire chief. But they said they didn't see it, and the fire chief said it might be a gas leak."

"What kind of gas looks like green fog?" Sammie asked.

"Exactly what my dad said. Do you guys think my dad's crazy?"

Sammie and Rahul exchanged a glance.

"Not at all," Sammie said. "Actually, we think all this weird stuff is related too. And all the adults around here blow it off, like it's normal for hair to go purple with no dye, or for a cat to walk on the ceiling. But these things aren't normal!"

"You know what should be normal?" Ms. Dillwater stood above them, her arms crossed, and her eyes gigantic in her big glasses. "Students working on their assignment instead of wasting my class talking about nonsense." She looked over at Dylan, her face softening for maybe the first time ever. "I'm sorry about what happened to your house, Dylan, but let the adults figure all this out. Now finish with the potatoes and let's make science happen."

CHAPTER 3

THE NEXT SATURDAY, Sammie rode her bike around town on a beautiful day, spring finally breaking through the long Minnesota winter. Nothing odd had happened in days, which was odd in and of itself. She and Rahul hadn't gotten any closer to figuring out what happened to the Schumacher house. Ms. Dillwater had stopped any attempt they made during school of asking Dylan more about his father's theories.

Rahul had a big, extended family gathering at his house, so Sammie rode alone, bored. She didn't want to be home because her mom was in a mood, stressed about something that had happened at the bank that week. So Sammie rode in circles.

Bored and hungry, she headed for home, but she stopped just in front of it when she saw a man standing on the sidewalk staring at her house, a yellow lab on a leash stretching away from him. But the man stood still, examining the house with wide eyes.

At first Sammie didn't recognize him, but the curl in his light brown hair and the shape of his face reminded her of Dylan. She'd only seen him once or twice, but she was pretty sure it was Mr. Schumacher. He wore some athletic shorts and an old t-shirt. She'd only ever seen him in nicer clothes; maybe he, like Dylan, was still wearing what they wore on vacation.

After a few moments, he looked over, startled.

"Oh, hi there," he said. "Do you live here?"

"Yes. My name is Samantha Stadler."

"Sammie? I think I've heard my son Dylan talk about a girl named Sammie in his class."

She nodded, trying not to blush. Dylan had mentioned her by name? "Yeah, I know Dylan. Most people call me Sammie, but my mom hates it, so I start with Samantha."

He smiled. "My mom was the same way. My name is Matthew, but everyone calls me Matt, except for my mom and great aunt Clara." He turned and looked at the house. "How long have you lived in this house?"

"My whole life. My parents bought it from my dad's grandpa before he died. It's been in the family forever."

He nodded, looking back at the house. "Did you know your house is in the very center of the valley, as far as I can tell, between the lake, Lutheran Hill, and the river bend?"

"I didn't know that. How do you know that?"

He shrugged, the same gesture Dylan had repeated so often during their conversation earlier that week. "My head is filled with useless little facts."

Silence hung between them as Sammie looked at the ground and Mr. Schumacher continued staring at the house.

"I'm sorry about your house," Sammie said after a while.

"Oh, well, weird stuff happens in Malsman Lake, doesn't it?" He didn't look at her. "Heck, there's probably a decent shot the house reappears in a day or two like nothing happened."

Mostly, the strange happenings stayed. Mrs. Wilson's horns had come and gone, but Viking was still a lizard and not a dog, and Mrs. Crawford's cabbages still produced some of the best strawberries in the county. And Lutheran Hill was still empty.

"It was nice to meet you, Samantha Stadler," Mr. Schumacher said, tipping his head. He walked away toward the edge of town, his dog pulling him along.

Sammie stood there for some time watching him walk slowly away, her bike tilted so she could stand. She was pretty sure she'd never seen Mr. Schumacher walking his dog down her street before, and the hotel Dylan had mentioned they were staying at wasn't close by.

"Sammie!" her mother called from the front stoop. "Come on in. Let's get some lunch in you."

Sammie stashed her bike at the side of the house and

rushed inside.

Her mother had warmed up some roast beef from two nights prior and turned it into sandwiches. Colin was already seated on his chair, stuffing grapes into his mouth three at a time. Sammie hadn't realized how hungry she was until the smell of the re-heated dinner made her stomach rumble.

"Who was that outside, sweetheart?" Mom asked.

"Mr. Schumacher, Dylan's dad."

"Matt Schumacher?" Her mom looked past Sammie into the hallway as if she might get a look at the man. "That's awful what happened to their house. Crazy. I didn't even hear a storm that night. Slept right through it."

Sammie decided not to argue about the disappearing house. All Malsman Lake adults, except for maybe Mr. Schumacher and Sheriff Masters, ignored all the weird stuff, and Mom was the worst offender. Sammie swore that Colin could transform into a monkey and Mom would laugh it off and then drop the monkey off at daycare the next morning.

"Where's Dad?" Sammie asked.

"Had to run into work for a few hours. A pipe broke at the warehouse, and he's checking in on the repairs."

Sammie dove into her food and was halfway done with her sandwich when she noticed her mom wasn't eating anything, just checking her phone.

"Aren't you hungry, Mom?"

Mom looked up. "What, sweetheart?"

"Aren't you going to eat?"

She sighed and stuffed her phone into her pocket. "Not really hungry today. It's been a long couple of weeks."

"Not enough money to go around?" Sammie had heard her mother say that phrase a lot the last couple of years. Too many farmers needed loans, and too few got the money they needed.

"Yes. And the Schumacher house wasn't the only casualty the other night. The Hanson farm lost a silo and a barn. Gone, just like the Schumacher house."

Sammie set her sandwich down. "Just like the Schumacher house? No debris?"

Mom scrunched her face like she always did when Sammie said something outlandish. "No debris? I'm sure there was some debris in both cases." She shook her head and moved from the dining room into the kitchen.

"I'm done," Colin said, climbing down from his chair, his mouth packed with as much food as it could handle. He was really good at talking with his mouth full. "I'm going upstairs to play with my cars." He dashed from the room like his feet had wheels.

"Alright, nugget," Mom called, her voice moving from the kitchen over to her office as she spoke. Her office chair creaked and the sound of typing punctuated a rhythm similar to Colin's bare feet tramping up the stairs.

Sammie finished her sandwich, thinking about her

mother's report. The Hanson farm was pretty close to town, not that far from Lutheran Hill. She hadn't heard anything about it at school, probably because the Hansons were older and didn't have any kids left at home. A silo and a barn gone? It had to be connected, it just had to.

Just as Sammie was about to finish her last bite of sandwich, one of Colin's banshee screams spooked her. "I swear, Colin, if you're not almost dead. . ."

"Samantha!" Mom called from her office. "Can you go see what's bothering nugget?"

Sammie let go of an exasperated breath and headed upstairs. Colin was scared of everything, including bugs of any kind, his toys if they looked at him wrong, or even his blanket if it was piled up and looked like a dragon.

She found Colin at the door of their parents' bedroom, curled up and whimpering.

"What is your problem?" Sammie said.

"Closet. Something scary in my closet."

Sammie rolled her eyes. "There better be the biggest monster you've ever seen in that closet, Colin, or I'm going to--"

"Not big." He shook his head vigorously, his blonde hair flopping back and forth. "Not very big, but very scary."

Great, Sammie thought, *a daddy long leg or maybe a Japanese beetle. Such scary monsters.*

"Stay here, you big baby," she said. "I'll take care of your little, scary monster."

She turned and headed for his room, but stopped just inside his door. She couldn't see his closet from that angle, but she could see green mist.

The green mist had the same color and consistency as what she and Rahul had seen in the Schumacher's basement, and it pulsed with fluorescent green light. But unlike the unnaturally still mist they'd seen there, this mist moved, emanating from Colin's closet and filling the room like fog rolling off Malsman Lake.

Sammie's heart jumped in her chest as she tried to breathe, but struggled to. That green mist, possibly the same thing responsible for destroying Dylan's house, was filling her brother's bedroom. Most of her wanted to scream even louder than Dylan had and to run from the house, taking Mom and Colin with her before their house disappeared into nothing.

But something urged her forward. Colin had talked about a monster, not a cloud of green. Something was in his room, in his closet, and it could be the source of all the weird. She had to see it, had to know what it was. So despite the part of her brain screaming at her to run from the house like a gazelle from a cheetah, she inched her feet slowly forward.

As she moved to face Colin's closet, she could see that the mist definitely came from there. It was flowing slower now, like dry ice fog at a haunted house; that made it even creepier, if that was possible.

She faced his closet, but it wasn't really a closet anymore. A wide open space, like a massive corn field, filled the place where his underwear, pajamas and clothes should have been. But it wasn't a field, but more like a green sky, pulsing with the same light that illuminated the mist. And floating in the middle of the endless green sky was Colin's not very big monster.

Sammie wasn't sure how big the creature was. It looked small, but the space in the closet seemed to stretch forever backward, so maybe it was just far away. She also found it hard to describe. It looked like an eggplant sitting on a dozen spaghetti noodles. Its body was purple and shiny. The top of it was green, like the top of an eggplant but more like hair. It had no eyes, mouth or ears that she could see. And its spaghetti limbs moved like string in a breeze and didn't seem to be connected to its body.

It was the scariest freaking thing Sammie had ever seen in her life, and she immediately felt terrible for making fun of Colin for being scared. She only didn't scream because she was too scared to make a sound.

"Who dares to disturb Tal-Shah-Farneree Tublat." A voice rang out, with a sound like a thousand screaming babies. Sammie reached up to cover her ears, but her hands never made it there as her body shook with fear.

"Who disturbs the Emperor of Tublat?" the voice spoke again, just as menacing.

"Samantha Stadler," she whispered, surprised she could even squeeze the words out.

"What is a 'Samantha Stadler'? Are you the master of Dimension One? Have you come to challenge my conquest?"

The master of Dimension One? Sammie couldn't even order a pizza on her own. "I'm just a kid," she managed to say.

"A kid? A child? How primitive. What are you doing at my portal, primitive child?"

Somehow she knew the voice came from the eggplant creature, though no mouth moved.

"This is my house. Your portal is in my brother's closet."

"Your brother? Is he the master of this dimension?"

"I don't think so. He's barely potty trained."

The voice went silent for a time, as if the eggplant were considering her.

"Samantha Stadler, will you bow before me and serve the Master of the Eighty-Four Dimensions?"

Sammie took a deep breath, trying to find some courage. "Did you destroy the Schumacher's house?"

"What is a 'Schumacher house'?" The voice sounded confused, like Mom did when Sammie tried to explain the plot of a Sideralis book.

"A building like this one, where people live. It disappeared."

"Ah, yes, there was a domicile we accidentally sucked

into Dimension Seventy-Three. Opening dimensional portals is always complicated. Yes, so very complicated."

"You destroyed my friend's house." Sammie balled up her fist and tried to keep her temper in check. "He's living in a hotel!"

"A hotel? Samantha Stadler, primitive child, I have no idea what you're talking about. But if this friend of yours is still alive, you should be grateful. A full dimensional portal reversal is quite dangerous. We lost seventeen Gahrstanzans just the other day trying to recreate the portal between Dimension Eighteen and Dimension Forty-Seven. Whatever a hotel is, it sounds quite preferable to the eternal blackness of death."

Gahrstanzans? Dimension Forty-Seven? Emperor Eggplant made as much sense to her as she seemed to make to him.

"Regardless, primitive, you should serve me. I plan on conquering your world, making it the eighty-fifth member of my empire. If I deem that your primitive race is worthy of assimilation, then I think you'll rather like it."

"And if we're not?"

Eggplant's spaghetti arms stopped waving. "Well, extermination is never pleasant."

Extermination? Did he mean their house, Malsman Lake, or was he talking about the whole world? This was no longer just picket fences changing colors or floating cotton candy.

"I won't let you exterminate our world," she said, her courage building.

The Eggplant Emperor laughed, a sound like a thousand fingers scraping a chalkboard. "My dear primitive Samantha Stadler, the difficult part was opening a portal to your dimension. I've been trying for some time now. But I've figured it out. Now that the portal is open, my influence will spread. And once the portal allows for full transference, well, your dimension will fall as did the eighty-three before it. Emperor Tal-Shah-Farneree Tublat, Master of the Eighty-Four Dimensions, has never failed in conquest. I will not fail now." He laughed again, and this time Sammie did cover her ears to try and keep the hackling sound from her brain.

What could she do? She had to get help, had to find a way to close the portal and stop Emperor Eggplant. But how? She didn't know anything about dimensional transference, or, well, dimensional anything.

But she decided to start simple. She stepped up to Colin's closet door and shut it. She doubted that would slow down a master of many dimensions, but it was the best she could think of.

She stepped back, expecting the door to fly open or get blasted open. But nothing happened. The mist in Colin's room began to evaporate and Sammie ran out to go find some help.

CHAPTER 4

Sammie ran from Colin's bedroom to find her brother still sitting at the door of their parents' room. He looked up when she came out, his eyes wide.

"Did you see the weird little monster?" he asked.

Sammie wasn't sure what to say. She didn't want to scare him, didn't want to add to the fears she knew he must be feeling. But she knew how it felt when no one believed you, and she wanted him to know that she did.

"I saw the little monster," she said after a moment. She crawled down onto the floor and cradled Colin into a big hug. He wrapped his arms around her neck.

"Come on," she said. "We need to get out of the house."

"Look!" Colin's eyes went wide again and he pointed up toward the ceiling outside of his room.

Sammie turned to see some green mist gathering there, pulsing with its vibrant light. It accumulated like a cloud, something like you might see on a cartoon right before a mini rainstorm unleashed its fury on an unsuspecting character. A green line formed in the middle, spreading slowly across the cloud. The florescent green line then grew fat, building up and down, until it assumed the shape of an open eye. Sammie shuddered.

"Is the cloud eye watching us?" Colin asked.

"Let's go." Sammie stood and gripped Colin's hand, pulling him down the stairs as fast as she could.

When they reached the bottom of the stairs, they nearly ran into their mother who was coming out of her office.

"Sammie," she said, "I was thinking of. . .are you two alright? You both looked like you've seen a ghost."

Sammie wanted to tell her mom what she'd seen, but how would she possibly get her mom to believe all that when she thought a Komodo dragon replacing a dog was not weird?

Hi Mom. Yeah, we're frightened because there's an Eggplant Emperor who's opened a portal in Colin's closet, and he's trying to take over the world. And our house might disappear like the Schumacher house did. Oh, and an evil green cloud eye was watching us.

"I thought you had a lot of work to do," Sammie said instead.

"Well, I need a break, and I was thinking of running to the store. Would you two like to come?"

Colin let go of Sammie's hand and then jumped into their mother's arms.

She swung him lovingly. "Oh, nugget, what's gotten in to you?" She squeezed him tight and smiled as she rested her head on his.

"I'd rather not go to the store," Sammie said, trying hard not to look up the stairs to see if the green cloud eye had followed them. "Can I stay here?"

Mom frowned as she set Colin down. He clung to her leg. "I'd rather you come with me."

"What if I rode over to Rahul's house and hung out there?"

"Doesn't Rahul's family have a party or something today?"

In all the commotion of the last few minutes, Sammie had forgotten about the party at Rahul's house. Rahul's brother was home from school in Boston, and the Patils had invited dozens of friends and family over. Sammie hadn't expected to see Rahul at all until the next day after church.

"He said they'd be wrapping up after lunch," she lied. These family parties at the Patil house usually lasted late into the evening.

"Alright, but have him or his mom text me that it's ok for you to be there. And don't get in the way. If they're cleaning up, offer to help."

Still wrapped around his mom's leg, Colin looked up the stairs. He shook like he did after a bad nightmare. Mom scooped him up into her arms and walked toward the garage.

"Let's go, little nugget. Maybe we'll get you some candy at the store." She carried him toward the garage.

"Stay out as long as you need!" Sammie called out after them. "Maybe get some ice cream or something." She knew that last phrase might get her into some trouble; Colin was absolutely addicted to ice cream and became unbearable once the idea got planted in his head until he got some. But Sammie needed them to be out of the house until she figured out what to do.

Sammie dashed into the front yard and was on her bike and zipping down the street before her mom even backed out of the driveway.

The space between her house and Rahul's house was less than a mile. The Patil family home was also older, though they had transformed the place. When Sammie's dad had gone there once a few years before, he'd complained for weeks afterwards about how the Patil family had gutted the place and taken away all of its charms. Sammie translated that as they had a kitchen that wasn't smaller than her bedroom and they had adequate closet space. Of course, none of the Patil closets likely housed a power-crazed eggplant.

She heard and smelled the Patil party before she saw it. The spicy sweet aromas of Indian food hit her as she turned onto his street, and the clanging music came with it. As she drew closer, she also heard voices clamoring above the sound of the Bluetooth speakers. Their house sat on the end of the street on a huge lot, a long lawn extending behind until it reached thick woods. The Patil house was on the very edge of town, and Lutheran Hill hung behind, looming like a bad omen.

She'd never actually seen one of these parties, though she'd heard Rahul describe them many times. The older folks were dressed in traditional, colorful clothing, the women in dress and pant combinations of orange, green and yellow. The outfits were amazing looking, with complicated embroidery around cuffs and sleeves. As the people got younger, they stuck less and less to the colorful dress. The few small kids, Rahul and the children of his older cousins, wore t-shirts and shorts or jeans. Some of the older cousins wore a colorful shirt that looked kind of like the traditional ones but over jeans or shorts.

Sammie put her bike down in the front lawn and approached the roaring party, but then stopped. It felt a lot like intruding. She'd been friends with Rahul for forever, but parts of their worlds did not cross over. She'd eaten lunch at his house and had come to enjoy the food, but now she was walking into something she hadn't been invited to.

"Hello, Samantha."

Sammie turned to face Rahul's mother, Lata. She was a tall woman with rich brown skin and long black hair. Her face was round like Rahul's, and her eyes were the kind that always seemed to see more than other people. She was a doctor, and, according to Rahul, somewhat famous in her field.

"Hello, Mrs. Patil." Sammie always felt like bowing in Lata's presence but resisted the urge.

"You can always call me Lata, Samantha. What brings you to our little party?" She spoke with an accent unlike any other resident of Malsman Lake besides her husband, but it was clear and beautiful. She almost sounded like she was singing.

What should she tell Lata? She was a lot less dismissive than Sammie's parents, and usually laughed when Rahul and Sammie had some odd theory about the List of Mysteries. But she was a doctor, a scientist, and she always wanted proof. How could she prove that an alien emperor lived in her brother's closet without taking Mrs. Patil there to see it?

"I was bored," was all she could manage to say, "and I forgot about the party."

Lata's eyebrows went up, clearly not believing a word Sammie said. Sammie wished she could sink out of the woman's sight.

"Rahul is in the back playing cricket," she said. "Follow me."

Sammie followed her in a half-trot to keep up with Lata's long strides.

Dozens of people filled their long lawn, and the music was loud, though the conversation, laughter and the crack of the cricket bat were even louder. Their party was nothing like anything that happened at Sammie's house or at the Lutheran church. When her extended family got together, it was more subdued. They'd grill hotdogs and hamburgers, some kids would throw a football around, and the adults would slowly get glassy-eyed with beer.

This party crackled with energy. The music thumped in a beat that seemed to demand dancing, and several younger women were doing just that. The men and women clustered together by gender and age, laughing, telling animated stories, and drinking. Some of the older folks sat on the side, amused looks on their faces as they watched the festivities.

Beyond the dancing, eating, and drinking, a group of a dozen or so boys and men played cricket. It seemed like chaos to Sammie, who barely knew the rules to American sports. One of them threw the ball on the ground and another swung a flat piece of wood at it. They all stopped as Lata and Sammie approached.

Sammie's eyes found Rahul far from the pitcher, standing bored near the woods. His eyes found her at the same time and widened with surprise. He ran toward her at full speed.

"Sammie," he said, breathing heavily. "What are you doing here?"

She looked between Rahul and his mother, not sure what to say. Her lie from before about forgetting about the party seemed absolutely silly now. "I need your help with something."

He nodded knowingly. "Well, I think this party is close to winding down."

"Our guests won't leave until after dark, Rahul," his mother said. "That's hours from now. And your father wants you to keep playing, I think."

Rahul looked back at his father. Sammie hadn't noticed before, but he was the person pitching, or bowling, or whatever it was called in cricket. Rahul's father, Gautam, was a thin man, gangly with a long face and a bushy mustache. He was a little shorter than his wife, and he always wore a serious expression. While Lata had always been friendly if a little distant, Gautam treated Sammie more like an unwanted pet. He was never rude, but he wasn't exactly nice either.

"Well, cricket isn't fun," Rahul said quietly, not meeting his mother's eyes.

"While I agree with you, the sport is quite important to your father. He will be sorely disappointed."

Rahul sighed, resigned to his fate.

"But, if Samantha really needs you." Lata turned to Sammie. "Is this very important?"

This question she could answer with full honesty. She stood tall and met Lata's eyes. "Yes, Mrs. Patil, very, very important."

Lata smiled, her teeth flashing and her eyes holding a

mischievousness Sammie had never seen. "Well, then, I guess Rahul must go. I will pacify my husband. But, Rahul, be back soon. And know that Papa will not be pleased."

Rahul bounced off the ground. "Of course, Ma. We won't be long."

They bounded away stopping by Rahul's garage to snag his bike.

"My mother must really like you," Rahul said as Sammie retrieved her bike from the front lawn.

"Why do you say that?" Sammie said as they rode away. "I thought maybe she didn't like me."

"Ma runs our house, there's no doubt about it, but the one thing she defers to Papa on is cricket and his boys. She never gets in the way of that."

"So if she likes me, why does she always look at me like I'm up to something?"

Rahul looked over as they turned onto her street. "She does? Hmm. I never noticed that." He paused a moment and looked up at her house. "So what's the emergency?"

She told Rahul everything she'd seen and her suspicions that the Eggplant Emperor was responsible for the Schumacher house, the old Lutheran church, and probably a lot more weirdness.

Rahul stood tall on his bike as she finished her story. "Well, your house is still there. That's a good sign, right?"

They pulled up in front of her house, and Sammie stopped her bike and didn't get any closer, dread filling her.

The Eggplant Emperor was in there, in Colin's closet, and that cloud eye was in there too. She didn't much feel like going back in.

Standing there reminded her of something she hadn't told Rahul.

"One more thing," she said. "Mr. Schumacher was here, staring at our house right before I found the dimension thing in Colin's room."

"What? Dylan's dad? What was he doing here?"

"Walking his dog, I guess, but it was weird. When I got to the house, he was just staring at it. Kind of creepy, actually."

"Do you think he's in league with this eggplant guy?" Rahul asked. "Maybe they tried opening the portal together at his house, but it didn't work."

"You think Dylan's dad is working with an alien from another dimension?"

Rahul sighed. "Probably not, but I don't know, it seems like a pretty big coincidence that he was standing out here staring right before you discovered that thing."

It had been very strange.

"So are we going to go check it out, or what?" Rahul asked, dropping his bike on the lawn and walking toward the front door.

"Rahul, stop." She dropped her bike and grabbed his arm. "A house disappeared because of this weirdo eggplant guy. What if we're in it when it disappears?"

Rahul stopped as if he hadn't considered that. "Well, what should we do? I mean, your mom is going to be coming back. What are you going to say to keep her out of the house?"

"Maybe we can say there's a gas leak?"

"And when she calls the gas company and they don't find anything? We'll be in big trouble."

"Better than being dead or moved to some weird eggplant dimension."

He considered that for a moment. "But didn't the eggplant guy say they'd figured out how to open the portal? Doesn't that mean it's stable?"

Sammie responded with an exasperated huff. "So I'm just supposed to believe whatever a strange vegetable floating in my brother's closet says?"

Rahul drew his lips into a thin line. "Good point. But what's our other option? Stand here and stare at the house like Mr. Schumacher and wait for your mom? We're the only two people in this town who believe anything strange is happening. We need to find out."

Sammie smiled despite the churning fear in her gut. "Now who sounds like they've been reading too many Sideralis Academy books? That's like something Andromeda would say."

Rahul rolled his eyes as hard as he could. "Whatever. So maybe those books are good for something. What would Andromeda Rodriguez do?"

Sammie knew exactly what her favorite character would do: she'd go inside and find out what was going on. She wouldn't wait for adults, wouldn't try and figure a way around it. Andromeda Rodriguez would solve the problem and save the day.

"Fine," she said, her face feeling flush from a stiff wave of nervousness. "Let's go check this out."

Rahul smiled and nodded. "That's the spirt." He rubbed his hands together. "Another dimension! This is going to be so cool."

Sammie did not feel even a fraction of his excitement, but she led the way anyhow.

She opened the front door, half expecting to see the cloud eye hanging there in the entryway, but there was nothing out of the ordinary. A pair of Colin's discarded socks sat near the stairs, and one of his toy cars sat on its side near her mom's office door. It looked entirely normal for the Stadler house.

"I almost grabbed your shoulders and said 'boo,'" Rahul said to break the silence.

"Good thing you didn't," she replied with narrowed eyes. "One of my boney elbows would have found your stomach."

She led the way upstairs, taking each step like it might unleash some dimensional terror. But besides a creak or two, they didn't hear or see anything. The normalness of it felt weird.

When they reached the landing, Sammie turned to look toward Colin's door. She could see the spot near the ceiling where the green cloud eye had watched her, but nothing was there now.

When they reached the top of the stairs, she stopped. "This is a really dumb idea."

"It's an eggplant with spaghetti arms," Rahul quipped. "What is it going to do? Serve us itself for dinner?"

"He's the emperor of eight-four dimensions, Rahul. He must have some weapons or soldiers or powers or something."

"Maybe he conquered the dimension of the potato trolls and the carrot elves."

Sammie glared at him, considering unleashing one of her boney elbows at him anyway.

"Fine, the Eggplant Emperor is terrifying. But standing out here isn't going to do us any good. Let's go see it." Rahul walked around her and into Colin's room.

Sammie followed close behind, almost hiding behind him. He hadn't heard the eggplant's creepy voice, hadn't seen the green eye. He didn't get how scary this was. She couldn't wait to see his terrified face after they opened the closet.

Colin's room seemed normal, his toddler bed a mess of blankets and a zoo of stuffed animals. His toys were scattered like they'd been tossed through a dimensional portal. But this was all normal in the room of a rambunctious boy.

Rahul faced the closet, ignoring the mess. "Well, it's time to have a look at this." He paused, his bravery from moments before seemingly gone.

"I'm sure he won't turn you into fries like he did to the potato trolls," Sammie whispered.

"Ha, ha." He looked back, no smile on his face. Then he turned, reached out, and pulled the closet open.

But there was no Eggplant Emperor, no sea of green energy, no voice like a monster with a megaphone. The closet held superhero underwear in a pile, a clothes basket surrounded by dirty clothes, and a half-eaten bag of BBQ potato chips Colin must have taken from the kitchen.

"I swear I saw it," Sammie said, stepping closer. "It was all here."

Rahul turned to her, not a sliver of doubt in his eyes. "I believe you, Sammie. But if your eggplant friend isn't in the closet anymore, where did he go?"

Two days later, Sammie sat in class as Ms. Dillwater droned on about something she found important, but the bored expressions of Sammie's classmates indicated that no one else did.

Sammie's eyes found Dylan, sitting halfway across the room. He looked over and their eyes met. He smiled a little. She blushed and looked down at her hands, clasped in her lap. She hoped the blushing hadn't been too obvious, but Rahul always said she looked like instant sunburn when she got embarrassed.

Rahul and Sammie had decided that they should tell Dylan about the eggplant guy, but they hadn't been given the chance over the past two days. Ms. Dillwater seemed extremely interested in keeping Rahul and Sammie away from Dylan, and their teacher had been extra crabby about conversation in class since spring break.

"Alright class." Ms. Dillwater raised her voice, and some of the half-sleepy eyes snapped back toward her, including Sammie. "It's time to transition to language arts. We seem to all be struggling quite mightily with grammar, so it's time for some more instruction to try and replace YouTube with some useful information."

It didn't take long for Sammie's mind to flutter away from Ms. Dillwater's discussion of abstract and concrete nouns. Even though she tried to think of something else, she kept thinking about the Eggplant Emperor. Was he really trying to take over the world? Was that even possible? The alien had floated in that green field, suspended like a puppet on strings. Could something without legs actually conquer earth?

He had said he was the master of eighty-four dimensions. How many dimensions were there? Was that why Malsman Lake was so weird? Did all those dimensions somehow affect her little town?

None of it really made sense. Not that she spent much time thinking about aliens, but if she did imagine them, they definitely didn't look like an eggplant on a pile of spaghetti. And of all the places for a dimension-conquering alien to appear, why did it have to be in her little brother's closet? Sammie loved the weird, but this was too weird and too close to home.

Poor Colin. He'd been sleeping on the floor in Sammie's room, something she wouldn't ordinarily agree to. But he didn't want anything to do with his room, and Sammie understood why. Heck, she didn't want to anything with Colin's room either.

"Miss Stadler, if you could please join us on planet Earth and leave wherever your mind is." Ms. Dillwater's sharp tone brought Sammie out of her imagination.

Sammie turned to find the entire class staring. Chloe Weathers and Emily Swanson sniggered at her. Rahul's face looked like he was talking about the Twins' latest catastrophic loss, and Dylan was looking at the floor.

"Yes, Ms. Dillwater?" Sammie said, her voice shaky.

"That was the third time I called your name, Samantha."

"Maybe she didn't hear," Dylan offered, looking up, "because we all call her Sammie."

Ms. Dillwater shot Dylan a harsh look, and his eyes moved back to the floor.

Their teacher turned back to Sammie. "Miss Stadler, please come see me at the end of the day."

Sammie spent the rest of the day with a nervous feeling in her stomach, kind of like when she'd broken her mom's favorite Christmas ornament and had been trying to figure out how to tell her. Sammie wasn't sure why she felt so bad. Sure, she hadn't been paying attention, but kids did that all the time; it wasn't like she'd stolen something or bullied someone.

At the end of the day, the rest of the class filed out of the room, and Sammie remained seated at her desk. Rahul was the last one to leave, hanging for a few moments by the door. He smiled a sympathetic smile, hoisted his book bag onto his shoulder, and left Sammie alone with Ms. Dillwater.

The cross woman regarded Sammie with her bug eyes, like a spider might look at its prey before it wraps it in silk and stores it on its web.

"You seem very distracted lately, Miss Stadler. Would you care to tell me why?"

My brother's closet contains a dimensional portal filled with a conquering alien eggplant, was the thought that came to her mind that she didn't say. "I don't know, Ms. Dillwater."

Her teacher sighed and took the glasses off. She rubbed her eyes. She looked a lot younger without the glasses. "You are a good student, Samantha, and usually a well-behaved one, but this week, you haven't been."

Sammie's anger started to boil, and she looked away, her lips drawn into a line. Sammie was a behavioral problem? Chloe and Emily talked constantly. Chris Shatner was always saying inappropriate things to make the boys laugh and to embarrass the girls. And Mya Summers never paid any attention, always seeming surprised when she realized anyone else was in the classroom. Sammie didn't do any of those things. Talking once in class and getting distracted were the least of the problems happening in fifth grade. Ms. Dillwater was being so unfair!

Ms. Dillwater put her glasses back on, stood, and walked around her desk. She reached the desk across from Sammie, pulled out the chair and took a seat. Despite being an adult, Ms. Dillwater was small enough that the chair did not look small underneath her.

"I think I know what's going on," she said with a smug grin. "You and Rahul love a mystery, and you're trying to figure out what happened to Dylan's house. Am I close?"

Sammie's anger grew hotter. She didn't want to admit that Ms. Dillwater had gotten close to the truth, so Sammie said nothing.

"I know you fancy yourselves as junior detectives," she said, her tone always condescending, "but this is a serious matter that you should leave to the police. You and Rahul should not be poking around this."

"The adults don't see the weird stuff," Sammie blurted out.

Ms. Dillwater did the most unexpected thing Sammie had seen from their teacher all year: she smiled. It wasn't the arrogant grin she usually flashed when proving them all wrong. It was an actual, genuine smile. It made her look young.

"Weird stuff? Samantha Stadler, what on earth are you talking about?"

Sammie wanted to spout out the dozens of weird things she knew, but she kept her lips tight. She wasn't going to play any games with Ms. Dillwater.

"Malsman Lake is one of the most boring places on the planet," Ms. Dillwater said. "Very little happens here. I think you and Rahul have too big of imaginations."

"A house disappeared," Sammie said, meeting Ms. Dillwater's eyes with a glare of her own. "No debris. No reason. That seems pretty weird to me."

Ms. Dillwater sat back in the small chair. "I think there are many reasonable explanations, Samantha. And it's not your concern. You don't need to worry yourselves about the Schumacher house, or weird things, or green mists. You should just be kids and behave."

She stood and walked to the front of the room, sitting behind her desk. "You are excused. In the future, please try and pay attention in my class."

Sammie sat there for a moment, stunned. Then she gathered her things and hurried from the classroom. Sammie and Rahul had said nothing about the green mists, but, somehow, Ms. Dillwater knew about them.

▭

Sammie lay in her bed, her mind racing and sleep avoiding her.

Sammie had wanted to talk with Rahul about her strange conversation with Ms. Dillwater, but he'd already been gone when she came out of class, picked up by his parents. She had tried to call him earlier in the evening, but he hadn't answered his phone; he sometimes forgot where it was.

The room was dark, save for the soft glow of Sammie's night light. Sammie looked up at the ceiling, the fake sky above her shining with the dim light of the constellation stickers her father had put up there years ago. Colin breathed heavily, having fallen asleep quickly despite his objections that he wasn't at all tired. But Sammie couldn't sleep.

Was Ms. Dillwater somehow involved in this? Sammie could almost hear Rahul's voice inside her head, saying that their teacher seemed like the type to be the henchman of a conquering eggplant. Why was she pushing for Rahul and Sammie to stop investigating things unless she was working for the deranged vegetable?

Nothing made sense, even more so than usual in a town that often didn't make sense.

She looked down at Colin. Mom and Dad thought his fear of his bedroom was normal, just something that happened to kids sometimes. Maybe they were right about it seeming normal. Sammie had been afraid of shadows in her bedroom when she'd been younger, and she had spent some anxious nights on the floor of her parents' room. But Colin's fears weren't driven by a crazy imagination; her little brother had really seen a monster in his closet and a floating eyeball in a cloud. The thought of both made Sammie shudder despite being covered by a super warm blanket.

Sammie wasn't sure what time it was or how long she'd been trying to fall asleep. She starting drifting finally, her eyes closed, and her mind finally letting go of eggplants and other dimensions.

Sammie sat up in bed, her eyes snapping open. Voices fluttered down the hall, too quiet for her to make out the words. At first, she wondered if it was her parents. They were both night owls, staying up and doing things long after Colin and Sammie went to bed. But as she concentrated on the voices, she knew it wasn't them. Both voices sounded like men.

She laid back town, turning her back to the sound. Maybe Ms. Dillwater was right. Maybe Sammie should leave all this alone. What could she possibly do against a dimension-conquering emperor? He had hinted that he commanded armies or something; Sammie couldn't even get her little brother to do what she wanted most of the time.

She closed her eyes, but she knew sleep wouldn't come. Maybe her dad had someone over and they were chatting downstairs.

She sat up again, pushing the blankets aside. She offered a quick prayer for safety. She didn't pray much, but she thought it might help in confronting an eggplant alien.

She stepped over Colin and held onto her doorknob, taking a deep breath.

Please say that dad had a friend over and that I'm going

to open this door and hear two old guys talking about the Minnesota Vikings or the Minnesota Gophers.

She opened the door and immediately knew it wasn't her dad. The house below was completely dark, and the door to her parents room was shut, no light coming from the bottom. But there was light in the hallway, a sickly green light coming from Colin's open bedroom door.

And the voice's weren't talking about football. Sammie recognized one of the voices. It was the nails-on-stone sound of the Eggplant Emperor.

Still, Sammie couldn't make out all the words. She wanted to shut her door and climb back into bed. Or maybe she should wake up her mom and dad. Wouldn't they have to notice Colin's glowing green closet and the alien voices? They couldn't dismiss something like this, right?

But she knew they would. Grownups ignored everything around here. Maybe Sheriff Masters would see it as weird, but Sammie didn't dare call the cops. If the green light and conversation were gone before they arrived, she would be in super big trouble.

Ms. Dillwater had been wrong. It wasn't up to the adults to save Malsman Lake; it was up to Sammie Stadler and Rahul Patil.

She crept away from her doorway and toward Colin's room. She got near the door and stopped, the voices finally clear.

"I don't like those cats either, Tublat," an unfamiliar

voice said. It sounded very normal, very human. Sammie decided not to look around the corner to try and catch a glimpse of whoever the new guy was. "But invading Dimension One is really stupid. You'll get a war."

"War is my goal, Jadirel Trum," the Eggplant Emperor said, his inhuman voice sending more chills down Sammie's back. "I cower before no one, not even the Dimensionera. And this is none of your business. You are a fool and a prisoner. The Master of Eighty-Four Dimensions does not take orders from the likes of you!"

"Before you get too frosted, your misshapenness, this is my dimension now."

Eggplant laughed his crying-baby laugh. "You cannot stop me, Jadirel Trum. And once I have control of Dimension One, I will find your little prison and insure you never leave."

"I'd like to see you try, dipstick. How long before I pull out the welcome wagon?"

"I understand little of what you say, Jadirel Trum. This simple language is clunky."

The other person, Jadirel Trum, sighed. "You're as thick as my granny's glasses. When is your invasion?"

"Nine days in this dimension's time. Then the portal will be strong enough to bring my army through. Cower before me, Dimension One!"

The green light disappeared, and all went dark and silent. Sammie froze. Was this Jadirel Trum going to walk out of Colin's room? Who was he, anyway? But no one came out and nothing moved. She waited for a few minutes and then crept back into her room. She shut the door behind her, stepped over Colin, and climbed back into bed.

Nine days. Sammie and Rahul had nine days to find out how to stop the Eggplant Emperor from conquering Malsman Lake.

CHAPTER 6

THE NEXT MORNING, Sammie called Rahul's house first thing and told him to be early to school so they could chat.

"What am I supposed to tell my mom?" Rahul asked.

"Tell her you forgot about a group project meeting. She'll believe you forgot."

"Hey!" he protested. "I don't always forget stuff."

They met early at school and Sammie told him everything, about her weird conversation with Ms. Dillwater, and about the conversation she'd overheard in Colin's bedroom.

"That's crazy!" Rahul said when she finished. "Who's this Jadirel Trum dude? Think he's a good guy?"

Sammie laughed. "I thought this wasn't a Sideralis book, Rahul, with good guys and villains."

He rolled his eyes. "Fine. Maybe it's like one of those books. But it would be nice if we had some help. And do you think Ms. Dillwater is working with the eggplant guy? Maybe she's helping him open these portals."

"You think our teacher is helping an alien invade Malsman Lake?"

He shrugged. "Why not? She hates all of us. Maybe this is her revenge against bratty fifth-graders. Why else would she tell you not to keep digging? And why would she know about green mist? We need to keep an eye on her."

Sammie wasn't convinced Ms. Dillwater was helping the Eggplant Emperor, but their teacher had been strange yesterday.

The bell rang and they hurried to class. But Ms. Dillwater was not there. A neatly dressed man stood in front of the class, his tall, wide frame a complete opposite to the tiny Ms. Dillwater.

Sammie and Rahul hustled in, the last two to arrive.

"My name is Clarence Manswander," he said as the class settled. "You can call me Mr. Manswander or Mr. M."

"Where is Ms. Dillwater?" asked Madison, one of the girls who particularly liked to ignore Sammie.

"Ms. Dillwater has gone away," Mr. M said, his voice a bit too high for a man his size. He had too little hair on his head, but he made up for it with a bushy mustache. "I will be your teacher until she returns."

"When will she return?" Dylan asked.

Mr. M scrunched up his face like it had been a particularly hard question. "The principal did not give me that information. And, unfortunately, Ms. Dillwater did not leave behind good notes, so I don't really know where to begin."

The rest of that morning was spent with Mr. M trying to get to know them and figure out what they'd been learning. Some of the students, including Sammie and Rahul, tried to help by telling Mr. M what Ms. Dillwater had taught recently. But others, like Gavin Hunter and Hunter Pillman (Rahul called them the Hunters), lied about it. They glared at anyone who told the truth, so most kids stopped talking. Rahul, as usual, did not.

"That's weird about Ms. Dillwater," Sammie said to Rahul as they made their way onto the field for recess.

"Super suspicious the day after she tells you to stop investigating everything." Rahul twirled a fallen little branch like a sword. "She's either sick, woke up this morning realizing she hates kids, or she's off helping her eggplant master."

"We need to get out to the Hanson farm," Sammie replied. "We need to find out what happened, see if we can find anything."

Rahul nodded. "Yeah, let's do that tomorrow. I'll take pictures this time, and we'll--"

"Hey, India," Hunter said, approaching them quickly with Gavin in tow.

Rahul turned to face the two bigger boys. "What do you want, Hunter?"

"I want you to keep your smelly mouth shut." Hunter never missed a chance to make fun of the fragrant Indian food Rahul liked to bring for lunch.

"I wasn't even talking to you," Rahul said, still defiant despite the size difference. Hunter and Gavin both played just about every sport, and Gavin excelled at hockey.

"We mean in the class," Gavin said. "We have that idiot Mr. M for the next little while. Let's keep him confused for as long as possible. Don't help him out."

"Some of us like to learn, Gavin," Sammie said.

Gavin smiled at her and looked back at Rahul. "Do you need your girlfriend to stick up for you? Is that what they do in your country?"

"America is my country, you moron," Rahul shot back, his hands balling into fists. "I was born in Minnesota, same as you two knuckleheads. And I can name the starting lineup for the Twins. Can you?"

Hunter stepped closer, and Rahul stepped back a bit. "Watch your mouth. And who cares about the losing Twins? I root for the Yankees."

"Figures," Rahul muttered.

"What's that?" Hunter got really close now, his face almost touching Rahul's.

The smaller boy did not flinch. "I said it figures," he said even louder, "since you're a complete bandwagon guy anyway. You probably like the Lakers and the Patriots too."

Hunter shoved Rahul, and he fell onto his back, kicking

up a little dirt as he did.

Sammie rushed to his side. "Stop it!"

"Shut up, nerd," Gavin breathed. "We don't usually pick on girls, but we could do something new today."

Sammie looked down at her friend. He had dirt all over him, and he was nursing skinned hands. He looked on the edge of tears, a fact the Hunters were going to be sure to point out.

"Leave him alone, Hunter." Dylan walked up behind Rahul, his eyes tight.

"Stay out of this, Schu," Gavin said. All the boys, besides Rahul, had nicknames for each other, like Schu for Dylan Schumacher, Hunter for Gavin Hunter, Carl for Logan Carlson, and so forth. Most boys lacked a proper imagination.

"I said leave him alone." Dylan was their match physically, and by the look on his face, he wasn't going to back down.

Gavin glared at him, but Hunter pulled on his friend's arm, eyeing a teacher who seemed to be paying close attention. "Come on, man, before these do-gooders get us in trouble."

Gavin gave each of them another glare and turned away.

"I guess I shouldn't have called him a moron," Rahul said, pulling himself to his feet. "I didn't think he'd understand what it meant."

"Hunter used to be cool before he started hanging out with Gavin," Dylan said. "And moron is not that hard of a word. I would have gone with imbecile."

Rahul huffed a laugh. "Thanks, man. You didn't have to do that."

"I know. But you two are the only two who have said anything about my house. Everyone else pretends I'm not living in a hotel and that my entire freaking house didn't just disappear. Even the teachers. Sometimes I hate this town."

Those were the most words Sammie had ever heard Dylan say. He was just so quiet usually.

"It's not so bad, once you get past the imbeciles," Rahul said. "I mean, we even have the biggest Sideralis Academy fan in the world right here." He pointed at Sammie.

Her eyes went wide and she suppressed the urge to push Rahul back to the ground. She hoped she wasn't blushing too much.

"I love those books," Dylan said, looking at the ground. "It was cool in my old school to like them."

"Not so much, here," Sammie said. "What domus are you in?" She regretted the question immediately. How geeky did she really need to prove herself to be?

Dylan looked up and smiled. "Umbra."

"I hate to break up this fascinating geek fest," Rahul interjected, even though he'd started it, "but how are you and your family doing?"

Dylan shrugged. "Fine, I guess. Dad is wiggin' out. He called in sick all week, pouring over maps of the county and stuff. Mom says he's having the weirdest midlife crisis ever. I think he's just trying to figure out what happened."

"Who's your favorite Sideralis character?" Sammie blurted out before she could contain the question.

Dylan smiled again, half-laughing. "I like Kaito a lot. I think he's like me."

Kaito was one of the main character's friends. He was from Japan and athletic and soft spoken. It fit pretty well.

"Sammie saw your dad on Saturday," Rahul threw in with a smirk.

"Really? Where did you see my dad?"

I saw him stalking my house right before I found a crazy alien in my brother's closet. (She couldn't say that.)

"He was walking your dog in front of my house," she said instead. "I recognized him because you look alike."

Dylan wrinkled his nose. "Really? I don't think we look much alike."

"Everyone thinks I look like my dad," Rahul responded. "And my mom. And my brother. But that's only because you are all pale and think all Indians look exactly the same."

After a slight pause, Dylan started laughing and the other two joined. "I didn't know you were so funny, Rahul."

"Please don't encourage him," Sammie pleaded.

"What were the imbeciles bothering you about?"

Rahul shook his head. "They want to confuse Mr. M. They didn't want me helping him."

Dylan looked back at their school building. "What happened to Ms. Dillwater?"

"Maybe she just got sick," Sammie suggested.

Dylan took a deep breath. "Nothing normal happens in Malsman Lake. I'm guessing it's something really weird."

Sammie wanted to tell him about the Eggplant Emperor and the other dimension, but she just couldn't. He liked Sideralis Academy, and even if his favorite character wasn't Andromeda, Kaito was pretty cool too. But dogs turning into lizards and vegetables turning into fruit was not the same as a potential alien world takeover.

The bell rang, indicating the end of recess, which always felt too short, especially that day.

"Catch you too geeks later," Dylan said, sprinting back toward the school. He'd called them geeks, but it felt endearing as he smiled back at them, not the insult it was often meant to be.

"I never thought I'd say this," Rahul said, "but I think Dylan Schumacher is a cool guy."

"You only say that because he laughed at your jokes."

"'Who is your favorite Sideralis character'?" he replied in his best Sammie imitation.

She blushed as they walked toward the building. "Yeah, well, not my best moment."

"He's right about Ms. Dillwater," Rahul replied.

"Nothing normal happens here. After what she said to you yesterday, this has to be connected. We need to go to the Hanson farm, and we need to find out what happened to Ms. Dillwater."

"How would we do that? It's not like either of us know Ms. Dillwater out of school or anything."

"I know where she lives."

Sammie stopped. "What? How?"

Rahul smiled and kept walking. Sammie jogged to catch up.

"She's not far from my house. Mom goes a bit overboard on first impressions. We took some Kala Jamun over to her house after she moved in." He rolled his eyes. "I had no idea that the nice woman who answered the door would turn out to be our greatest enemy." He paused. "Well, our greatest enemy until an evil eggplant showed up in your house."

"So what should we do?" Sammie asked. "Bring her some more Indian desserts?"

As they stepped inside, a broad smile stretched across Rahul's face. "That's exactly what we'll do. We'll take her some get-well treats. Then we can find out what's really going on."

━━━

Saturday morning, Sammie decided to ride her bike to Lutheran Hill. She needed to get out of the house as it had become insufferable the past couple of days. Colin was in a mood, whining and crying anytime he didn't get his way, which meant that her parents gave in to almost all his requests. And mom's stress level continued to be high, which made everyone in the house, except for maybe Colin, walk on eggshells.

Rahul was spending the morning making a treat with his mom for Ms. Dillwater. It was the perfect cover for visiting their teacher. If she was just sick or out of town, it wouldn't be strange. But if something weird was happening, they might be able to get a good look at it. Rahul had confirmed last night that Ms. Dillwater's house had not disappeared, which had come as mild disappointment to them both.

From Lutheran Hill, Sammie could see the Hanson farm. The old stone grain silo and the weathered red barn were landmarks along the county road heading north out of town. Both buildings were gone, just like the Schumacher house. The only thing left of the silo was a stone foundation. It was jagged, like a giant had torn the structure above it off. And the only sign of the old barn was a barn-sized patch of dirt in the middle of a grassy field.

What had the Eggplant Emperor said? That opening up dimensional portals was difficult? Had they tried and failed at the Schumacher house and then tried at the Hanson farm? Did that mean that if it hadn't worked in Colin's closet that their house would have torn away as well? The

Eggplant Emperor had said that the Schumacher house got sucked into another dimension. Did that mean that all their stuff was safe and sound in some strange place, with eggplant-like aliens now wearing Dylan's clothes and playing with his sisters' dolls?

Even for Malsman Lake, this seemed like too much weird.

As Sammie turned to go, she looked back at the lake and stopped, dropping her bike. The bright morning sun shimmered on the smooth surface of the lake, the light dancing with the slight breeze, and a green mist hovered over it. It looked exactly as it had a few years back when she'd noticed it and her parents hadn't. This time, she felt drawn to the lake, like she should get on her bike and go there right now and take a swim. The lake was calling to her.

But that was ridiculous. It was March in Minnesota. The lake had only recently unfrozen and would be freezing cold. And Rahul would be waiting for her to deliver their spy treats to Ms. Dillwater.

Sammie looked down and picked her bike back up. When she looked back at the lake, the green mist was gone as if she'd imagined it. And maybe she had. When you were constantly looking for weird, sometimes it came only in your mind.

But no. She'd seen it, and she'd felt something weird. No, she would not be like the rest of Malsman Lake and ignore what was happening.

She biked as hard as she could toward Rahul's house, hoping he and his mom were done with Ms. Dillwater's treats.

⬛

If Rahul's mom thought it was suspicious that two kids who didn't really seem to like Ms. Dillwater wanted to bring her some treats because she might be sick, she didn't give any indication. She seemed to be proud of them and said to Rahul, twice, as they prepared to walk over to their teacher's house, just how much she'd enjoyed spending the morning with him.

They had considered a hundred alternatives on how they could use the treats to spy on Ms. Dillwater. Rahul had suggested putting some kind of listening device in the sweets or on the plate, but they could not figure out how to do that without it being obvious or without Ms. Dillwater swallowing the microphone. Plus, they didn't have any spy equipment anyway.

They had also thought of trying to drop something once they got in the house. But drop what? Sammie had suggested Colin's old baby monitor, and for a while, they had felt really good about the idea. But the thing didn't recharge anymore, and it was prone to weird noises, which would give them away. And they'd also have to be close enough to the house, which meant hiding nearby.

So they would have to settle for learning what they could when they dropped off the treat.

Even wrapped in tinfoil, Sammie could smell the sugary sweetness of the patisas. Rahul's mom had set some aside for them, which they had gobbled up before leaving.

As they walked, Sammie filled Rahul in on seeing more green mist over the lake.

"This can't all be coincidence," Rahul said after Sammie finished her story. "I mean, Ms. Dillwater is probably like eggplant guy's official evil spymaster. She tried to get you to stop because she knew you knew!"

"Ms. Dillwater, an evil spymaster? Seems like acting like an evil witch lady isn't a great spy cover."

Rahul narrowed his eyes. "That's what makes it such a perfect cover. People who are too nice are suspicious. But a mean lady like Ms. Dillwater would be perfect."

Sammie wasn't sure she agreed with his reasoning. They lived in Minnesota -- the perfect cover would be to be nice like everyone else. There wasn't a 'too-nice' in Malsman Lake.

"She's from Milwaukee," Sammie replied. "People are mean in Milwaukee."

Rahul fixed her with a narrow glare. "How do you know? How many times have you been to Milwaukee?"

She'd only been once when she was as little as Colin, but Rahul knew that already. So she said nothing.

They stopped in front of a small, narrow house with a

porch facing the street. The lawn was still brown from the winter and the bushes in the front were only starting to show some buds. It looked like a perfectly normal Malsman Lake house, not the lair of an evil spymaster. Maybe Rahul was right about the cover.

"We'll find out soon enough," Rahul said.

They marched up the short walkway and onto the porch. Sammie rang the doorbell.

As they waited, she looked over at the small driveway. A small, detached garage, that was nearly as big as the house, sat at the end of the driveway. An old Honda Civic was parked in the driveway.

"Maybe she's not home," Rahul said, his face curved in frustration.

"Her car is here," Sammie said, pointing at the Honda.

"How do know that's her car?" Rahul pointed out.

"Not sure," she replied, "but I recognize it. It's parked in the school parking lot every day."

"Leave it to you to recognize cars." He shook his head. Rahul did not understand how Sammie recognized the make and model of every car they passed. To him, a Honda and a Hyundai were the same. But that was ridiculous. Sammie's father loved to talk about cars, and Sammie had always found them interesting as well.

"Maybe she's too sick to answer the door," Sammie offered.

"Maybe." Rahul stepped to the side and looked in a

window. His eyes widened, and he looked back at Sammie. "Look at this."

Sammie stepped up next to him and looked through the dirty window. At first, it just looked like a cluttered sitting room, but as she looked closer, it wasn't just cluttered; it was trashed. One of the couches was turned upside-down. A flower pot sat overturned, its dirt spilled onto the carpet. A lampshade was missing on a tall lamp and wasn't anywhere to be seen.

A deep knot formed in Sammie's stomach. Maybe this wasn't the normal Malsman weird; maybe this was just something bad.

"Somebody came here looking for something," Rahul said. "We were right! Ms. Dillwater was involved in something." He jumped off the porch and onto the driveway, still clutching his plate of patisas. "Come on. Let's check it out."

Before Sammie could object, Rahul darted around toward the back of the house. Sammie jumped off the porch and followed him around the house and to a back door. He stood their facing it, his mouth open a little. The back door sat ajar just a little.

"We should go get Sherriff Masters," Sammie whispered.

"Nonsense," Rahul replied. "I'm just going to step in and leave these treats in her kitchen with a nice note."

And again, before Sammie could object, Rahul stepped inside Ms. Dillwater's house.

CHAPTER 7

Sammie wanted to throw the tinfoil-covered plate at the back of Rahul's head as she slipped through the door and into a small kitchen. But before she could even say anything, she froze. The room was just as big a mess as the front room. Most of the drawers were open, their contents gone or dumped onto the floor. The kitchen table chairs were laying on their sides, and the kitchen table was gone. A lone lamp shade sat by the sink, maybe the one that had been missing from the other room.

"What happened to this house?" Sammie muttered.

Rahul set his plate on the counter and started looking around.

"What are you doing?" Sammie protested.

He turned to face her. "Investigating. Isn't that why we're here?"

Sammie looked at all the chaos. "But what if whoever

did all this is still in the house?"

Rahul paused, as if he hadn't considered the possibility. He looked around like whoever did this might jump out of the adjoining hallway. "But Ms. Dillwater has been gone for a few days."

"Yeah, but we don't know when this happened." Sammie looked around, trying to see if anything gave away how long the kitchen had been like this. But despite it being a kitchen, there was no food spread anywhere.

She stepped over the fridge and opened it. Everything looked in place; not a ton of food, but from what Rahul had said, Ms. Dillwater lived by herself. There were a few left-over containers, a half-gallon of milk, a small carton of eggs, and other assorted normal fridge things.

"I guess whoever trashed her place wasn't hungry," Rahul said from over her shoulder.

Sammie moved over to the only unopened cupboard and found shelves full of canned goods and dry pasta. Again, it had been left alone.

"If they were looking for something, why not look for it with the food?" Sammie said, keeping her voice at a whisper. She was still pretty sure being in here was a bad idea. "I'm not saying it's a great place to hide something, but it is a place."

"Maybe they found what they were looking for before they reached the food," Rahul offered, his tone indicating he didn't believe his own hypothesis.

Every drawer had been opened. The front room had been turned upside down. But all the food sat in its proper place like the rest of the house hadn't been turned into a clean freak's greatest nightmare.

Rahul moved toward the hallway.

"Where are you going?" she asked.

He looked back at her. "To check out the rest of the house."

Sammie took a deep breath and followed him, not sure if it was because she didn't like the thought of him being alone in this creepy place or if she was too scared to be alone herself.

The hallway mirrored the two rooms they'd seen, random objects scattered along its edges: some clothes, a small lamp, and what look like the contents of a desk. Two doorways lined the walls, one on each side. Rahul approached the first door slowly, like a bad spy from a movie, tiptoeing dramatically. He stopped in the doorway.

Sammie came up behind him. The small bathroom looked as crazy as the other spaces. A tube of toothpaste sat on the floor, half emptied into the tile. Toilet paper ringed the shower like a teenager might have decorated a friend's lawn. The mess made no sense; it didn't even appear as if they had been looking for something.

"What happened in here?" Rahul asked, mirroring Sammie's thoughts.

"I think we need to leave." Sammie couldn't stop the

sinking feeling in her stomach. This all felt wrong. Maybe it was related to the weird; maybe it was something else. But she didn't want to stay there any longer.

"Let's check the rest of the house," Rahul pleaded. "Maybe she's hurt somewhere here in the house by herself. We can help."

Rahul turned to lead the way and Sammie followed, but then they both stopped. Green mist poured from the next open door, floating toward the ceiling. It came together in a cloud, just like Sammie had seen in the hallway outside Colin's room. A bright green line of light formed in the middle of the growing cloud, opening to reveal an eye. The sinking feeling in Sammie's gut moved, spreading its dreadful fear across her whole body.

"Is that the green eye you and Colin saw?" Rahul asked, his voice finally a whisper.

"Yes." She gripped his arm, still holding her treats in the other hand. "Can we go now, please?"

Rahul nodded, and then turn and ran from the house.

▭

As they ran, Rahul whimpered, kind of like Colin had the day he saw the eggplant guy in his closet. Rahul looked back at the house once, but Sammie did not look back; she didn't want to know if the green eye was following them.

They reached Rahul's house in record time, gasping for breath. For once, Rahul had kept pace with her.

"Mother!" Rahul called as they entered. "Mother! We need your help!"

"Mom ran to the store," came the voice of Rahul's older sister, Sumera, who was visiting for the weekend. "She'll be back soon."

"Come on." Rahul pulled on Sammie's arm. "We'll go tell your parents. We have to tell an adult."

"Sumera is an adult."

He rolled his eyes. "No she's not. She'll never believe anything we say. And what is she going to do, torture the green eye with Taylor Swift?"

Sammie looked in the direction of Sumera's voice, but Rahul was right. This was time for adults, not a college kid.

"Holy crap," Rahul said as he picked up his bike and got ready to ride. "Our world is being invaded! We need to tell someone." He looked scared, his face pale, his eyes wide.

"Didn't you believe me before?"

"Of course I believed you. It's just, seeing that creepy eye for myself..." He shivered. "Well, it's really scary, Sammie. We need help."

Sammie picked up her bike. "My parents won't believe us. They won't believe the green eye or the Eggplant Emperor."

"They don't need to," Rahul said. "We just tell them the rest. We went to drop off some treats to Ms. Dillwater, and we saw through the front window that the house was trashed."

Sammie nodded. That would work; her parents couldn't ignore that.

They raced toward the Stadler home, Sammie leading but Rahul keeping much closer than usual.

They dumped their bikes in the front yard and ran into the house.

"Mom! Dad!" Sammie called. "Where are you?"

She came to stop in the kitchen, her parents sitting at the table, mugs in hand. They both looked up as Sammie and Rahul raced into the kitchen.

"What's going on, Sammie?" her father asked. They both smiled at the same time.

Sammie didn't respond. Their smiles. Something was weird with their smiles. Dad had a goofy, crooked grin, not a toothy, full smile like usual. And Mom didn't smile much lately. Her face looked relaxed, like when they were on vacation. What was in those mugs? Happy juice?

"Hi, Mr. Stadler, Mrs. Stadler," Rahul said through gasping breaths, and their overly grinny smiles turned to him. "We have something important to tell you. We went to deliver treats to Ms. Dillwater, because, well, she might be sick and stuff, and when we got there, her house was totally trashed, like the mob had wanted something from her. So yeah, we think she might be in trouble."

Sammie wasn't exactly sure how she expected her

parents to react, but their reaction shocked her. Both of their faces went from false happy into deep scowls.

"What were you doing at that house?" Sammie's dad asked.

"And why did you look inside?" Sammie's mom added as soon as her dad finished his question.

"Rahul told you," Sammie said, hesitating. "Ms. Dillwater hasn't been in school. We heard she might be sick or something, so we were going to take her some treats."

Sammie's parents loved that kind of thing. Mom was always baking cookies to take to friends, and her dad often made his famous lasagna whenever someone at their church got sick or had someone in their family die.

"You should mind your own business," Sammie's mom said, her eyes narrow.

"And leave poor Ms. Dillwater alone," Sammie's dad added, his eyes matching his wife's.

Rahul stepped up closer to Sammie's parents. "Did you hear what I said?" The question was disrespectful, especially for Rahul, but his panic had worn down his politeness. "Ms. Dillwater's house is trashed. At minimum, we should call the police. I mean, she could be in trouble or something."

Both of their faces turned back to the earlier smiles.

"Go and play, children," Sammie's dad said.

"Have fun and don't worry about all this other stuff," Sammie's mom counseled.

They both took a drink from their mugs in perfect unison.

Rahul looked over, his face folded in confusion. It was Sammie's turn to shrug.

"Where's Colin?" Sammie asked.

"Here's upstairs in his room," Sammie's mom said.

"He's eating some ice cream," Sammie's dad said.

"Come on," Sammie whispered, pulling on Rahul's arm.

She led them upstairs, wanting to run but feeling too stunned. Rahul matched her slow pace.

"What's wrong with your parents?" Rahul asked, again using a whisper.

"Mom's been under a lot of stress," was all Sammie could say.

"That didn't seem like stress."

Sammie knew he was right. Her parents should have responded differently. Her dad was a fixer--he would have jumped up and driven his truck to Ms. Dillwater's house. Her mom was a rule-follower--she would have called Sheriff Masters. But neither of them had done anything they typically would do.

They found Colin in his room, sitting there in the middle, eating a gigantic bowl of ice cream. Much of it had melted, and Colin was covered in ice cream, across his shirt and face, chocolate and vanilla both, the melted stuff at the bottom a rich brown. The bowl was one that mom usually used to serve a big salad.

"Colin, what are you doing?" Sammie asked.

He smiled, his cheeks covered in ice cream. Some had even landed on the carpet. "Eating ice cream."

Sammie put one hand on a hip. "Mom let you eat ice cream in your room?"

He giggled. "Yes. She even said I should." He lifted the bowl up to his face. "She even gave me this. Two ice creams."

"How much ice cream did you eat?" Rahul asked.

"Two ice creams!"

"Like two cartons?" Sammie asked.

Colin just smiled and giggled again.

"Holy crap," Rahul exclaimed. "I need whatever is happening to your parents to happen to mine. Maybe I could get a Nintendo Switch."

Sammie's parents had a habit of giving into Colin, but not like this, not two cartons of ice cream in a salad bowl; the kid would be bouncing off the walls for a week with that much sugar.

"We need to go tell Sumera or hope your mom is home," Sammie said.

"And I thought this town couldn't get any weirder," Rahul said as they headed back to his house.

Sammie shivered. What was going on in Malsman Lake? And what was happening to her parents?

CHAPTER 8

WHEN THEY ARRIVED at Rahul's house, his mother's Volvo was back in the driveway and they found Mrs. Patil in the kitchen unloading some groceries.

"How did dropping off the patisas go?" she asked as they walked it.

Both of them hesitated, looking at each other and back at her, smiling nervously. Lata smiled like she often did, half amused, half serious.

So they told their story, interrupting each other with certain details. They even said they'd gone into the kitchen, but they left out exploring the rest of the house and the green eye.

Lata's face went serious as they spoke, but not into the sneer Sammie's parents had flashed.

"You shouldn't have gone into the house," she scolded as they finished. "Come."

They followed her out of the house and she walked quickly toward Ms. Dillwater's house, Sammie and Rahul trailing behind. Lata was tall, a little taller than her husband, and she always moved like she really needed to be wherever it was she was going. This time, Sammie figured, she really did.

The scene at Ms. Dillwater's house had changed since they left. Two Malsman Lake Police cars were parked there, one in the driveway and the other on the street. Sheriff Masters was standing on the front porch talking with a neighbor, an older woman Sammie recognized but couldn't name.

Rahul and Sammie slowed as they approached, but Lata did not, her fierce stride now directed right at the sheriff.

"We might be in trouble," Rahul whispered as they started walking again.

"Why? The sheriff will see what we saw." But Sammie's words were contradicted by a nervousness settling over her like a layer of ice.

"Since when do grown-ups in this town ever see anything?"

Lata walked up to the house, and Sheriff Masters turned to her.

"Good morning, Mrs. Patil. What brings you here?"

Lata stopped at the bottom of the steps, glancing back at Rahul and Sammie. "Maybe the same reason you are here, Vera. My son and his friend have something to tell you."

Sheriff smiled at the older woman, who nodded and walked away. She then turned her full attention and her deep green eyes on them. "What do you two have to tell me?"

Rahul looked at Sammie and nodded toward Sheriff Masters. Not so brave now.

"We came over to drop some treats off for Ms. Dillwater," Sammie said, each word having a hard time escaping. "We heard from our substitute teacher that she might be sick."

Sheriff Masters raised an eyebrow. "And then what?"

Sammie looked at Rahul, but his mouth remained closed. She sighed. "We went around the back and the door was open, so we went inside. But not very far! And then we saw that the house was a wreck and we left. We went to tell my parents, but, well, they didn't believe us, so we went to tell Mrs. Patil."

Sheriff Master's face folded into confusion. "Wrecked? How?"

"Stuff was everywhere," Rahul finally added. "Like trashed, like somebody was trying to mess it all up on purpose."

"You need to go inside and check if she's ok," Sammie pleaded. "I mean, we left, we were scared."

Sheriff Masters stepped down from the porch and bent

down to come eye to eye. But she didn't look mad or worried, just maybe a little confused. "Ms. Dillwater is in Milwaukee looking after her sick mother," the sheriff said. "She emailed me and asked that I look after her house. She also let the school know. So the sub was mistaken. She's not sick; her mother is."

"Oh," Sammie said, now confused herself.

"But what about her house?" Rahul asked.

Sheriff Masters looked back at the house and then back at the kids. "I went inside myself; the house is fine." She stood and turned to Lata. "The station got an anonymous call an hour ago from someone who saw two kids breaking into the house through the back."

"They didn't mean to break in," Lata said, her voice calm but firm. "It was just two kids trying to do something nice for their teacher."

The sheriff smiled. "I know. We found a warm plate of treats on the kitchen counter. They look delicious."

"You and your team can have them, Sheriff. They are called patisas. It's a family recipe."

The conversation was interrupted by one of the sheriff's officers coming around the house. He was younger, tall, and had a crooked smile. "Nothing out of ordinary, Sheriff. I locked the back door."

"Thanks, Collins. You can go."

He nodded at the sheriff and then again at Lata with a tip of his broad-brimmed hat, then left.

"But the house was wrecked," Rahul muttered.

Sheriff Masters laughed. "A little dirty maybe, but not wrecked. I think you guys got spooked. No biggie. It was nice of you to think of Matilda."

"Matilda?" Sammie questioned.

"Ms. Dillwater," Sheriff Masters clarified. "I'm sure she would have appreciated that."

"But the back door was open," Rahul muttered again.

Sheriff Masters ignored Rahul and turned back to Lata. "Have a nice day, Mrs. Patil."

"You too, Vera."

Sammie stood next to Rahul, as equally stunned. The house was not wrecked. Ms. Dillwater was in Milwaukee. Everything that had seemed so clear an hour ago now seemed as cloudy as can be.

"Come, children." Lata turned and walked back to the house, slower this time.

Sammie matched her pace, a different feeling filling her: embarrassment. Had they really seen everything they thought they had? And even if they had, who would believe them now about the Eggplant Emperor?

Lata looked down at her son. "You did not help Samantha at all with the sheriff. Typical of a man to leave a woman to answer the tough questions."

"She's not a woman, and Sammie--"

Lata stopped and faced her son, her stern expression ending whatever he was going to say. "I have taught you better than that, Rahul Patil. Let me guess: it was your idea to go into the house, wasn't it?"

He looked at the ground, completely cowed. "Yes, Mother."

"And yet, Sammie was the one who had to tell the sheriff about that. Why is that? You were brave enough to go into a house you shouldn't have, but not brave enough to take responsibility?" Lata took a deep breath and her face softened. "I am not really mad at you, Rahul. Just be a better friend. And I don't think you two did anything wrong."

"But who called the police?" Sammie asked, the question springing to her mind.

"The sheriff said it was anonymous," Rahul's mother explained. "That means they don't know."

"Her backyard is completely surrounded by trees, and it backs onto the park," Sammie continued. "Who would have seen us? I mean, they might have seen us go around to the back, but how did they see us go into the house?"

Lata smiled. "You are a smart girl, Sammie. I have no doubt you could lead the police department today."

"Mom is not a big fan of Sheriff Masters," Rahul added.

His mother shot him another sharp glance. "Sheriff Masters is fine. I just disagree with those who believe power comes from a gun and muscles." She looked like she wanted to say more, but she didn't.

Lata continued walking, and Sammie followed. Something felt wrong. Moments ago, she'd felt guilty and ashamed. But why? There was an emperor in her brother's closet who wanted to conquer the world. Even if Ms. Dillwater was in Milwaukee, her house had been trashed and the green eye cloud had been there.

Sammie just had to figure out how all this fit together.

⌑

The day wore on and Sammie stayed at Rahul's house, not wanting to go back and confront whatever was happening with her parents. She wanted to talk with Lata about it, but that window closed when Rahul's father returned home and heard about them going in Ms. Dillwater's house.

"What on earth was my child doing going into a stranger's house?" Mr. Patil's anger wasn't fiery like when Sammie's mom lost it, but more subdued. Despite being older than Sammie's own dad, Mr. Patil looked younger, some lines at his eyes, but not a speck of gray in his hair.

"I told you, Gautam," Lata said, rubbing her forehead, "they were taking treats over. I helped the kids make them. It was a nice gesture."

Despite his wife's pleading, he looked at Rahul with narrow eyes and then turned his gaze on Sammie. "Maybe he's spending too much time with the girl. He should be playing with other boys."

Lata's lips went thin. "Gautam, that is not appropriate to

say in front of the children. I will not have that discussion here and now."

Sammie looked down at her shoes. She'd always suspected Rahul's father felt that way; heck, most of the town saw their friendship as strange: the Indian boy and the blond girl. In a town where one day all the calendars lost the number two and a cat had lived on a ceiling for nearly a year, apparently Rahul and Sammie hanging out was the weird thing.

"Why don't you two go play some games," Lata encouraged, bringing Sammie out of her shoe stare.

"Rahul should be practicing cricket," his father said.

Lata pointedly did not look at her husband. "Go on. Have some fun. Forget all this nonsense."

Sammie followed Rahul up the stairs to his bedroom. He slammed the door, his face as angry as Sammie had ever seen it.

"Father is a jerk," he said.

Sammie couldn't disagree, so she said nothing.

"Sumera said dad ignored her. Didn't seem to have any interest in her, being a girl and all. But Akrit and I get all of his stupid attention."

"Do your parents fight a lot?" Sammie asked.

His face softened some. "Not really. They just don't talk much. Mother would never say it, but I think she's against arranged marriages because of Father."

"Their marriage was arranged?" Sammie couldn't even

imagine that. Her parents had been high school sweethearts right here in Malsman Lake. Her mother's parents had met at a church dance in Rochester. Her father's parents had met in college. Love was supposed to just happen.

"Kind of. My mother's parents would have let her say no, but it had been a thing since they were little." He shook his head. "Who cares about my family? We saw a freaking green cloud eye at Ms. Dillwater's house! Holy crap! And you know what's even stranger than that? Her first name is Matilda!"

Sammie laughed. "That's weirder than green mist turning into a cloud and then growing a glowing eye?"

"Maybe not. But Ms. Dillwater isn't much older than Akrit." Rahul's older brother Akrit lived in Boston and was in graduate school. "Nobody that age is named Matilda. It's not a name."

"People name their kids weird things all the time." But as she said it, she felt that it was all wrong. Everything about Ms. Dillwater, her house, and the story about Milwaukee, was wrong. A young teacher who hated kids. Young teachers were usually the coolest, but she acted like an old, crabby teacher stuck in a young woman's body.

Sammie sat in Rahul's desk chair and opened up a web browser.

"What are you doing?" her friend asked.

"Finding Matilda Dillwater."

A quick internet search turned up only two Matilda Dill-waters. The first one was familiar. The only photo was the same one on the wall of the school: big glasses, black hair, brown skin, brown eyes and a severe look like she was about to lecture students on their laziness. The other was an older woman, white hair, blue eyes, and glasses as big as the younger version. Sammie clicked on a link to the Greater Milwaukee School District and found out the older Matilda Dillwater was a retired elementary school teacher. The older woman also had an Instagram and Facebook account and showed up in a news story about her retirement five years ago.

Going back to the search page, she clicked on the only link that connected to the younger woman they knew: the announcement of her becoming a teacher at Malsman Lake Elementary. No social media, no high school achievements, nothing in college. The announcement said she came from Milwaukee where she'd been a teacher in the Greater Milwaukee School District.

Sammie sat back in her chair.

"It makes no sense." Rahul had been hovering over her shoulder during her search. "If she's a spy for eggplant dude, that's the worst cover ever. She picked a name only one other person in the world has. Try typing in my name. There's like a million Rahul Patils. She should be like Jennifer Smith or something."

"And both Matilda Dillwaters taught at the same

district in Milwaukee? Maybe the older woman is her mother."

Rahul reached over and clicked to the announcement of the older Ms. Dillwater's retirement, scrolling down to the bottom.

Ms. Dillwater was joined at her retirement party by her two sons, Robert Dillwater of Neenah and Kyle Dillwater of Chicago, and her six grandchildren.

"It makes no sense," Sammie said.

"She's not Matilda Dillwater," Rahul said, almost bouncing with realization. "She's an imposter. I bet she's not even human! She's an eggplant in disguise!" His face looked as excited as when the Twins had made the playoffs the year before.

"But what do we do about it?" Sammie asked. "I mean, Sheriff Masters is worried. Your mom, who believed us, is no longer worried, and my parents..." What was happening with her parents?

"We need more information," Rahul said. "We should break into Ms. Dillwater's house again. Or should I call her the eggplant witch?"

Sammie swiveled the chair around. "Are you nuts? We can't do that. We had a good excuse this time and everyone laughed it off. They won't next time. And somebody is watching the house. Remember the anonymous call?"

Rahul frowned. "And the green eye was there. I wonder if that thing can hurt us?"

Sammie shivered at the thought of encountering that thing again. It hadn't done anything to anyone yet, but it was about as creepy as it got.

"So what do we do now?" she asked.

Neither of them could offer a good answer.

CHAPTER 9

By Wednesday of the next week, neither Sammie nor Rahul had a clue what to do, but they knew they only had a few more days before the Eggplant Emperor invaded their dimension. It felt like the world might be ending, and Sammie was frustrated she couldn't do anything. Her hero Andromeda Rodriguez would have known what to do.

Her parents had returned to normal. Her mother was stressed about work, and her father piddled around the house with his projects. No more talking in concert or getting mad about weird things. Or giving Colin salad bowls of ice cream.

Sammie had asked her mom about the ice cream, really just to gauge her mother's response.

"Oh, that little rascal," her mother had said. "He must have pulled it out of the freezer in the garage."

"He said you gave it to him."

Her mother had laughed. "You believed a four-year-old? He's on a strict no-ice-cream policy right now."

But somehow Sammie didn't believe it. Colin was too short to get into the outside freezer, and the salad bowls were high on the shelf--Sammie couldn't even reach them without the step stool, and then just barely. So either her mom was lying, or she didn't remember. Neither possibility made Sammie feel very good.

The other oddity of the week had been Dylan not coming to school.

"Maybe they're looking for a new house or something," Rahul had said.

But neither of them had a good way of contacting him. Sammie didn't have a smart phone or social media, and Rahul and Dylan had just recently become friendly. Sammie thought Dylan might have a phone, but she wasn't sure. She had considered going out to the hotel after school one day, but that had seemed too much like a stalker. She'd already been so awkward about his love of Sideralis Academy.

Wednesday afternoon, Sammie was in Colin's room looking at his latest drawings. Just two weeks before, she'd been ready to toss her little brother out a window. Now they spent most of their time together, even outside of Colin sharing her room at night.

"What do you think of this one?" Colin held up his latest drawing.

Sammie recognized it easily: purple body, green top on its head, and dozens of squiggly lines for limbs. What had he called himself? Tal-Shah-something? Master of the eight-four dimensions?

"That's really good." And it was. She knew kids twice his age who didn't have Colin's ability at art. The lines were rough and the detail scarce, but he had a good eye for shape and color.

He set the drawing back on his little table, shuddering. "Do you think he's still in my closet?" He started returning into his room now, but just during the day. And he hadn't opened the closet even once.

But Sammie had, several times since she'd overheard that weird conversation between the Eggplant Emperor and that someone else. But the closet had been normal each time. "Maybe he got stuck in the forty-fifth dimension or something."

Her brother nodded seriously as if she'd given a proper explanation. She wasn't sure she had any good explanations for any of this. And even knowing Ms. Dillwater's disappearance might have something to do with it, she and Rahul had come no closer to cracking that mystery.

They were interrupted by a knock on the front door. With mom busy working and dad piddling in the garage, she decided to answer it.

"I'll be right back," she told Colin.

He jumped to his feet. "Can I come with you?"

Her instinct was to say no, that he was being annoying. But instead she replied, "Sure."

Colin followed her out of the room.

She stopped on the landing when she heard the door open and her mother's voice. "Hello. Can I help you?"

"Yeah," came a tentative voice she's recognized as Dylan Schumacher. "Is Samantha here?"

Sammie peered around the corner wall and saw her mom standing with her hand on the doorknob and Dylan shuffling his feet on the porch. His eyes were red and he looked like he'd been crying.

She pulled back. Why was Dylan crying? She wasn't sure why, but she felt bad seeing him like that, like she shouldn't see him crying. But why? Everyone cried when they were hurt or very sad, and Dylan's life was a bit of a mess at the moment, so why shouldn't he be able to cry?

"Who are you?" Mom's voice changed, going cold and monotone. Mom was always polite to strangers, always. But that wasn't very polite.

"Dylan Schumacher," he said. "I'm in Samantha's class at school."

The sound of Dad's work boots echoed in the hall as he walked in from the garage. "Samantha is not here," he said, his voice unfriendly. Dad never called her Samantha. He'd given her the nickname Sammie. And he hadn't even been in the room when Dylan asked his question.

"When will she be back?" Dylan asked.

"She's very busy," Mom said.

"Lots of work," Dad added, speaking in concert like they had on Saturday.

"Please don't come back," Mom said sternly.

"Samantha is not your friend," Dad shot at the boy.

The door closer without a goodbye.

Sammie could hardly breathe. Saturday's exchange had been strange, but parents were sometimes strange. This had been different. Why had Dad come in from working in the garage? Why had they been so rude to Dylan? They knew what his family was going through. Mom always helped others, especially if they were in trouble. Instead, Mom had rudely turned away a boy crying on her porch. Shannon Stadler would never do that. And her dad loved cheering people up, trying too hard sometimes to get a person to smile when they were sad.

Sammie waited for her parents to walk away.

"What's wrong with Mom and Dad?" Colin asked, his face more curious than scared. He probably didn't understand the conversation they'd just heard, but he could feel it.

"I don't know." Sammie found she could barely speak. What was wrong with her parents? What had the Eggplant Emperor said? His influence would spread. Had he somehow taken over her parents? Was that even possible?

Sammie knelt down next to Colin. "I need to go someplace. Can you go play in my room until I get back?"

"Can I play with your Sideralix stuff?" He couldn't say Sideralis correctly.

Even with their newfound closeness, she didn't want to let him. Her Sideralis Academy toys and memorabilia were her most precious possessions.

But she had to go fast. "You bet. Have fun."

Colin sprinted toward her room.

Sammie turned and walked down the stairs as silently as she could. If her parents were brainwashed, then they probably wouldn't want her chasing after Dylan. But she had to help him; he had looked like he needed a friend.

She reached the door and pulled it open, slowly rotating the doorknob so it wouldn't click. Taps from Mom's computer came from the next room, and Sammie couldn't hear her dad. She stepped outside and closed the door behind her.

She found Dylan walking away from the house toward town, his hands in his pockets, his pace slow, his feet barely clearing the pavement.

She ran up to him, glad he hadn't sped away on a bike. But of course he hadn't; his house had disappeared and he wouldn't even have a bike to ride.

"Dylan!" she called as she approached.

He turned. His eyes were puffier, redder, and brimming with tears. Sammie wasn't sure she'd ever seen anyone so sad.

He pulled his hands from his pockets and wiped his

eyes, his face reddening with embarrassment. "I don't think your parents want you out here."

"I'm sorry about that." She stopped close to him, frowning. "I don't know what's gotten into them."

He shrugged. "Whatever."

"But just in case, let's go for a walk."

He nodded, and they continued slowly away from Sammie's house.

The spring sun was setting, casting long shadows from the neighboring houses and the tall old trees lining the street. Everything was green, birds chirped, and the sounds of kids playing in a nearby backyard floated on the soft wind. But it didn't feel like spring to Sammie; spring usually meant happiness, and she didn't feel very happy right at that moment.

"Why did you come by?" she asked.

He shrugged again. "I don't know. Wasn't sure who else to go to."

They walked another block in silence before Sammie spoke again. "What's the matter, Dylan?"

He didn't meet her eyes and kept walking. "My dad. My dad is missing." He paused to keep the tears from overwhelming him. "He's been missing since Saturday. He left in the morning to take the dog for a walk but..." He stifled a sob. "He hasn't come back."

Without thinking, Sammie reached out and hugged

him. He stopped and cried, burying his head on her shoulder.

After a few moments, he stepped away. "Sorry for being such a blubbering baby."

She smiled. "You should have seen me after I finished Caverns of Destiny." Caverns of Destiny was the tenth and final book in the Sideralis Academy series. "I cried for like a week straight, and it's not even real. This seems like a really good reason to be a blubbering baby."

This broke his sadness a little, his eyes brightening just a tad. "Yeah, that was a sad finish, but I won't admit to crying."

"So are they looking for your dad?"

He shuffled his feet and nodded. "Sheriff Masters has been out at the house a couple times every day. They found Buster, our dog, with his leash still on, out by our old house. But the only other clue they have is that someone says they saw him and the dog that morning on Poplar Street."

Sammie gasped. "Poplar? Where on Poplar?"

He raised his eyebrows. "What does that matter?"

Poplar Street was one down from Hillside Road, Rahul's street. Sammie was almost positive it was the road where Ms. Dillwater's house was, though she didn't know street names that well.

"I was on Poplar Saturday afternoon," she finally managed to say. "Rahul and I took some treats over to Ms. Dillwater's house."

Dylan's face pulled up into surprise. "You took Ms. Dill-water treats? You two can't stand her. Why would you take her treats?"

Sammie blushed a little. Was it that obvious how much they disliked Ms. Dillwater? "We were investigating. We thought Ms. Dillwater's disappearance was weird, even for Malsman Lake."

Dylan looked up, his eyes wide. "You saw something weird, didn't you?"

She nodded and started to walk again. Dylan kept pace as she told him everything about what they'd seen that day. Then she explained everything they knew, about seeing the Eggplant Emperor, the green cloud eye, her parents being weird, and the fact that Ms. Dillwater was probably not Matilda Dillwater from Milwaukee.

When she finished her story, Dylan did not look at her like she was crazy. He looked shocked, maybe a little scared, but she could tell he believed. "Dad thought something strange was going on. He said this town was weird, that there was a strange energy. He even told Mom and I he'd seen that green mist you're talking about."

"He's seen the mist?!"

Dylan nodded enthusiastically. "I believed him, but Mom thought he was going a little crazy. She even told Sheriff Masters that he'd become, what was the word, unsta-ble? They think he's had some kind of mental breakdown."

Sammie remembered the morning she'd met the

Eggplant Emperor. Dylan's father had been outside her house, staring at it, saying her place was in the exact center of the small valley. So she told Dylan about her conversation with his dad.

"He knew something," he replied. "He knew something bad was happening. I don't know how, but he knew. And he knew your house was part of it."

Sammie was sure he was right. If only Rahul and Sammie had confided in Dylan or his father earlier.

"Do you think he was at Ms. Dillwater's house?" Dylan asked.

"I can't say for sure," Sammie said, "but it seems like too much of a coincidence. He must have been there. If he knew about my house, maybe he knew something about Ms. Dillwater."

"I never liked her," Dylan growled. "If she hurt my dad..."

Sammie thought it out in her mind. Maybe Dylan's dad had gone into the house looking for evidence or something. Maybe Mr. Schumacher had trashed it trying to figure out something about the woman who was most certainly not named Matilda Dillwater.

"How's your family doing?" The question seemed like just the sort of thing her mom would have asked if she hadn't been acting so strangely.

"Mom's a mess," Dylan said. "The girls just cry all the time. No one knows what to do."

They walked for a while in silence, the sun falling lower and lower. They walked almost all the way to town.

"I should head back before my parents get even weirder," Sammie finally said, and they both stopped.

"What's wrong with them?"

Suddenly, Sammie felt like crying. What was wrong with them? "The Eggplant Emperor said something about his influence. I think he's done something to them."

"Like mind mites or something?" Mind mites were microscopic robots the villain in the Sideralis Academy books had used in book 5 to control the teachers.

"Something like that maybe." She looked away, her own tears forming.

"Can you help me find my dad?" he asked.

Sammie turned to look at him, wiping away her own tears. "I'm not sure where to start."

"You and Rahul know more about the weird stuff than anybody," he continued. "Who else is going to help? The sheriff? Teachers? If this eggplant guy has got my dad, then only you can help. No one else even knows he exists, and no adult in this stupid town will believe us." His eyes filled with tears again, and his lips twitched like he might start crying again.

Sammie wanted to help, but she had no idea how to. She had documented the weird stuff and collected the stories like other kids collected baseball cards or stuffed animals. She'd never imagined that there would be something like this, an alien who kidnapped adults and wanted to take over their dimension. They were just kids; how were they going to stop that?

Her hero, Andromeda Rodriguez, sprang to her mind. Even though it was just a book, she knew what Andromeda would have done. She had two best friends, Kaito and Henry. Sammie could be like her. If one of her good friends had asked for help, Andromeda Rodriguez would have said yes, she would have figured out how to solve the problem.

"I will try," she said, filling the words with as much courage as she could find inside herself.

Dylan's smile was small, but it made Sammie feel like she'd said the right thing.

"Meet me right here on Saturday morning," she said. "I should show you my closet."

He tilted his head. "Your closet?"

She wanted to slap her forehead. Had she just invited the cutest boy in school to her bedroom to look at her closet?

"It's where I keep my List of Mysteries," she said hurriedly. "It's got everything Rahul and I have ever discovered in there, including every time we've seen or heard of the green mist." She knew that she'd have to tell him about being in his basement; she wasn't looking forward to that.

Before she even knew what happened, Dylan reached over and gave her a quick hug. He blushed as he pulled back, looked at his shoes, and walked away at a near run.

"See you right here on Saturday," he called, looking back for only a moment.

Sammie tried to keep herself from blushing and turned back to walk home. She would help Dylan find his dad, and she'd figure out how to get the Eggplant Emperor's mind mites away from her parents. She had to, because she and her friends were the only ones who could.

But as she ran back to her house, a dark feeling dampened her enthusiasm. How on earth were they going to do that?

CHAPTER 10

AFTER TALKING WITH DYLAN, Sammie tried to keep her mind focused how she could help Dylan's dad, her parents, and maybe save the world. That seemed like a lot for a fifth grader.

But life kept getting in the way. Thursday and Friday in school were like torture. Times tables? Mesopotamia? Science? It all seemed so unimportant compared to keeping a crazy vegetable alien from taking over her dimension.

Her parents acted completely normal until Friday night when they announced, in their weird robotic synchronized voices, that they would be hosting a party on Sunday night for a bunch of their friends. When they said who would be coming, it seemed like a random list of people from town, not their usual close friends. For her mom, hosting a party seemed at least somewhat natural, but her dad hated going to parties, let alone hosting one. Sammie's father hated large groups of people, and it sounded like they'd invited fifty people! Sammie wasn't sure their old house could fit that many.

And they had invited Lata and Gautam Patil. It wasn't that Sammie's parents weren't friendly with the Patils, but they never associated with them outside of school events. The Patils did not attend Sammie's church, and most of her parents' friends came from church.

But the weirdest part was the lack of preparation for the party. Her parents didn't ask her to do any chores, and they didn't get a lot of food. They purchased some beer and wine and that was it. It didn't feel like much of party.

"Maybe the eggplant is trying to recruit more drones," Dylan had said to Sammie and Rahul Friday at recess.

"Or maybe he wants to get all his enemies together," Rahul had added. Really, none of them had any idea what the strange party meant. But it seemed important, and it made them more eager to do something.

On Thursday, Sammie had told Rahul about her conversation with Dylan. She had been afraid that Rahul would be annoyed, jealous, or skeptical. But he had only said, "We need to help Dylan find his dad before more people disappear."

They had considered moving their Saturday morning meeting to Rahul's house instead since Sammie's house was eggplant central, but all their strange evidence was in

Sammie's closet. So they met a few blocks from the Stadler house.

Getting into the house proved easy. Rahul had developed a complex plan of signals, distractions, and codewords. But as they approached Sammie's house, they saw her parents leaving in her mom's car. So they walked in with no trouble.

Once inside the empty house, they went up to Sammie's room and showed Dylan the List of Mysteries.

"Oh man." Dylan looked at all the scraps of paper, pictures and sticky notes and then turned to Rahul. "You really found a barking pig?"

Rahul nodded and smiled. "It was so weird. Apparently pigs kind of bark anyway, but this was totally different. The thing was still acting like a pig, but deep barks came out, like a big dog. My parents thought it was weird too. But the Callisters just looked out from the house and waved, as if the barking noises were normal."

Dylan pointed at a small handwritten note near the bottom of the closet door. "And I never heard about the garden gnomes that attacked the squirrels. You guys saw that?"

Sammie shook her head. "Nope. Mrs. Wilson, our third grade teacher, told us that story as if seeing inanimate fantasy creatures arm themselves to take out squirrels was just something that happens. Based on her story, we think that happened like twenty years ago."

She stepped into the closet. "All the ones marked with green had mist." She pointed at each one as she spoke. "The barking pig. The disappearance of St. Mark's church in 1911. I saw green mist a few years ago over the lake, and I saw it again the morning..." She looked over at Dylan. "The morning we went to Ms. Dillwater's place. Then we saw it in there."

She reached out and picked up an index card Dylan hadn't noticed. "And we saw it in your basement after your house disappeared."

Dylan looked between them. "You went to my house?"

"I was riding my bike to go meet Rahul near the lake, and I saw your house wasn't there," she said hurriedly. "And then..."

"And then we jumped into your basement, dude," Rahul finished. "Sorry, man. We weren't trying to be creepy or anything, but we had to see it."

Dylan looked at Sammie. She had been afraid he'd be mad or feel betrayed, but he only smiled. "That's how you knew I loved Sideralis Academy. You saw my stuff."

Sammie winced. "I'm sorry, I didn't mean to be a spy or anything, but..."

Dylan waved his hands. "Don't worry about it, Sammie. I don't care. I'm glad you saw it."

"Not to interrupt Comic Con here," Rahul interjected, "but now that we all know what we know, we should figure out how to do something about what's going on."

They spent the next hour coming up with ideas. Dylan thought they should camp out, twenty-four-seven, in Colin's room and wait for the closet to become a portal. Then they could take pictures and prove what was going on. Or maybe they could go inside the portal and look for his dad. The idea of stepping inside that closet filled Sammie with sinking dread.

Rahul's best idea was breaking back into Ms. Dillwater's house. He thought they could find clues. He was convinced that Ms. Dillwater had been acting as the Eggplant Emperor's spy, and Dylan agreed. But Sammie wasn't so sure. If she had been eggplant's spy, why had she disappeared? Shouldn't she be preparing for his imminent invasion?

"I think the lake is the key," Sammie said, looking into the closet. "On the morning after St. Mark's disappeared, there was mist on the lake. The morning Dylan's dad went missing, there was mist on the lake. I bet, if Rahul and me had made it to lake the morning we found your house, we would have seen mist on the lake too."

The boys were intrigued by the lake, but both wanted to pursue their own ideas, and they couldn't agree on what to do.

"I always think best with a freezie in my belly," Rahul declared when they couldn't break the stalemate. "Plus, Sammie's parents are going to be home any minute, and if they find Dylan here, they're likely to lock us all in Colin's closet."

So they rode bikes downtown to get freezies at Callister's Convenience Store. Dylan's bike had indeed disappeared when his house had, so he rode tandem with Rahul. They both said it would be weird if they rode with a girl, even though she was a better rider than both of them.

"Well, if you two bite it, don't blame me," she said with a giggle, imagining the two boys griping at each other if they did wreck.

They locked their bikes on the rack outside of Malsman Lake Library and walked into town. With a sunny, blue sky and warm weather, the town was buzzing with people. Winter coats had been shed, and while some wore light jackets, most just wore long sleeves. Some brave teenagers even wore short sleeves and shorts despite a slight chill.

Everyone seemed happy, shopping, eating, and chatting. Looking over at Dylan, Sammie could see that it bothered him. His dad was missing, his house had disappeared, and their dimension might get invaded that night. His face wore deep concern, worry, and sadness. And nobody in Malsman Lake seemed to notice.

"Let's get a freezie," Rahul declared a little too enthusiastically. Sammie winced, worried that Rahul's excitement might annoy Dylan, but the blonde-haired boy just smiled. Almost everything Rahul did seemed to amuse Dylan.

Callister's was busy but not full. They weaved through shoppers grabbing their energy drinks, beef jerky, and chips. The three friends made their way to the drink machine.

"Freezies," Rahul said again, speaking like he'd just discovered a new species of animal. "If there is a heaven, we shall drink freezies all day there while watching baseball."

"Baseball is boring," Dylan muttered absently, obviously not realizing the Rahul rant he had unleashed.

"Baseball is boring?!" Rahul turned on their new friend. "Baseball is the most intricate sport in creation, the perfect balance of action and tension--"

"I prefer football or hockey," Dylan said. "More action."

"You just don't understand baseball. If you understood it, you would love it." It was the same argument Rahul had used a thousand times with Sammie. He'd taught her the rules, how to recognized pitch types, and she could properly score a game by hand. And, though she never said it to Rahul, she still found it pretty boring.

"I've played baseball my whole life." Dylan looked down to the ground, any of the excitement from moments before fading back into sadness. "Dad likes baseball."

"Which flavor does everyone want?" Sammie asked, trying to re-focus the boys on freezies.

"There are six flavors," Rahul said, his voice reverent again. "Blazin' Blueberry, Raging Razberry, Killer Kola, Lucious Lime, Bouncing Bubblegum, and Chocolate Explosion. And so many combinations..."

Rahul did what he called the Crazy Ivan--all six flavors

in equal measure. Sammie got her usual Blazin' Blueberry and Raging Raspberry combo, and Dylan settled on Killer Kola. Sammie worried Rahul might critique Dylan's one-flavor choice (he always did), but he seemed to have sensed Dylan's mood and left it alone.

They wandered out Callister's and walked slowly down the street, all taking long sips from their massive freezie cups.

Dylan winced. "Brain freeze."

"Brain freeze is the best," Rahul responded, wincing as well.

"I wonder if Emperor Eggplant gets brain freeze," Dylan said.

"I didn't even see a mouth," Sammie replied. "I'm not sure if he even eats or how he eats."

"Evil masterminds don't deserve freezies," Rahul said with a wide grin.

"Don't all evil masterminds have a weakness?" Dylan offered.

Sammie considered it. "Isn't that superheroes? Like Superman and Kryptonite?"

"Super-villains usually have greed or something like that as a weakness," Rahul said between sips. He took another long drink. "But if he's got one, I bet it's fire. We'd turn him into the biggest eggplant parmesan the world--"

"Rahul! Dylan! Samantha!"

They all looked up at their names and saw Sheriff

Masters standing at the top of the stairs leading to the police station. They had wandered right past it as they walked.

"Funny you should all walk by together," she said. "I need a word with each of you. Would you mind coming inside?"

They looked at each other, their freezies momentarily forgotten.

CHAPTER 11

"DON'T you need a warrant or something to talk with us without our parents?" Rahul asked.

The sheriff laughed. "You're not under arrest or anything. I just wanted to talk with you about what you saw at Matilda Dillwater's house. And I needed to update Dylan." She looked at him with a sad smile. He looked away.

"Can we bring our freezies?" Sammie asked, not wanting to throw out a nearly full one.

Sheriff Masters laughed again. "Yes, I get one of those sometimes myself." Sammie couldn't imagine the stern police officer taking a long drink from the red straw and shaking her head at the brain freeze.

They followed her into the police station. Sammie had never been inside, and it was nothing like she'd imagined. If there was a jail, they didn't pass it. There was a front desk and then some cubes, like any other office, like a shabbier version of Sammie's mom's bank.

She led them to the back to a small office. It was as clean as any office Sammie had ever seen, to the point that it felt like no one used it. Sheriff Masters sat in an old chair behind a small metal desk. The three kids took seats opposite her, with their feet dangling above the floor.

Looking at Rahul and Sammie, the sheriff asked, "So what did you really see last week at Ms. Dillwater's house?"

They exchanged a look. Could they tell her about the green mist? Or the eyeball cloud?

Sammie looked back at Sheriff Masters. "Exactly what we said. The house was trashed. Looked like someone had been looking for something. But you said it just looked dirty."

The Sheriff sat back in her chair and looked past them. "Yeah, that's what I said."

Rahul sat forward on his chair. "You saw it! The house was trashed when you got there!"

She looked back at Rahul, her mouth curling into a smile on one side. "Lower your voice, Mr. Patil. You shouldn't accuse the sheriff of lying." Her slight grin faded as she looked at Dylan and then back at Sammie and Rahul. "I need you to tell me every detail about that house you can remember."

"We saw green mist," Sammie blurted out.

Dylan and Rahul looked over at her, eyes wide, but Sammie kept her gaze on Sheriff Masters.

"A green mist?" The sheriff did not sound like she believed Sammie.

"A green mist," Sammie repeated. "We saw it in Dylan's basement the day you found us there. And I've seen it before. Rahul saw it before once when the Callister's pig barked like a dog. Looks like fog, but it just sticks in place most of the time."

Sheriff Masters pulled a manilla folder out of a desk drawer. She set it in the middle of her clear desk. "Do you know what this is? It's my own little file on all the weird crap that happens in this little town. At least twelve incidents talk about green fog."

Sammie sat up. "Twelve? We only know of a handful."

The sheriff laughed and leaned forward on her desk. "Calm down, Detective Stadler. But it's only from outsiders and kids. No locals ever mention it. It's weird." She shook her head. "But let's get back to this weird day. Did you see anything else besides a messy house and strange green fog?"

Sammie wanted to tell her about the green cloud eye, about the Eggplant Emperor, about everything. But she just couldn't. Weird stuff? Sure, in this town, the chief of police had to know that. An invasion from another dimension? She'd think they were nuts.

"No, Sheriff."

The sheriff looked at Dylan. "Had your dad ever

mentioned Ms. Dillwater before? Do you know if they knew each other?"

Dylan shrugged. "I don't think so. I mentioned a few times how much I didn't like her, and Dad always talked about his third grade teacher, Mrs. Brown, and how she had reminded him of a troll. Mom didn't think it was funny." His mouth flinched into an almost smile but didn't quite get there.

"Do you think Ms. Dillwater and Dylan's dad are connected?" Rahul asked.

"She wasn't Matilda Dillwater," Sammie said.

"You should be a detective, Samantha." Sheriff Masters smiled. "I know. We don't know who that woman was, but we know she wasn't Matilda Dillwater. She disappeared the day I figured it out."

"So she didn't go to help her mother?" Rahul asked.

"That's what she told the school, and she emailed me to let me know she'd be out of town." She leaned back again. "I shouldn't be telling you kids any of this, but sometimes I think you are the only people in town who see that not everything is normal here." She took off her broad hat and ran a hand through her short brown hair. "Somedays I wish I'd stayed on the South Side."

"So what's the next step, Sheriff?" Rahul nearly bounced off his seat. "How can we help?"

She raised an eyebrow. "You can go home and stay out of trouble. That would help."

Rahul slumped back in his chair.

"Is Ms. Dillwater connected to my dad?" Dylan looked like he was on the edge of tears.

Sheriff Masters regarded him with a soft eye. "I don't know, son. I can't find any connection, but your dad was near her house last week before he disappeared. I promise, Dylan, I am looking. I will do everything I can to find your father."

Dylan nodded but looked away.

"Could you two boys step outside of my office for a bit?" the sheriff asked. "I need to talk to Sammie. Claire will have some candy for you at the front desk." She eyed their unfinished freezies. "Not that you need any more sugar."

The boys shuffled out, leaving Sammie alone with Sheriff Masters.

"Is everything alright at home?" she asked after the boys left.

The question caught Sammie completely off guard. "At home?"

"Yes. Is your family doing alright?"

Sammie looked down at her feet. What could she say about home? Mind mites? Aliens in her brother's closet? "Mom has been stressed out a lot lately," she said instead.

"Seems like a weird time to have a party," the sheriff said, "if she's stressed out."

"You know about the party?" Sammie couldn't let the

sheriff come to the party, especially if it really was some evil plot by the Eggplant Emperor.

She nodded. "Yes. It's a small town."

"You weren't invited?"

"Not much of party person, Samantha. And no."

"I'm sure it was a mistake." Her cheeks burned with embarrassment.

"Probably," the sheriff replied, not sounding like she thought it probable. "Have your parents been acting strangely?"

"Yes." Sammie tried not to cry. "Yes, they have been acting weird."

Sheriff Masters smiled, the kind of smile meant to make a kid feel better. It didn't.

"Stay out of trouble, Samantha Stadler. And if you need me, you know where to find me."

CHAPTER 12

"You know," Rahul said as they walked away from the police station, "it's possible that Sheriff Masters might be in on this too."

"Come on, dude," Dylan said. "She told us about Ms. Dillwater. She told us about the green mist. If she were part of the eggplant's army, why would she share all that with us?"

"That's exactly it," the other boy responded. "It's like a double, secret spy thing." But Rahul didn't seem like he'd even convinced himself of this crazy theory.

"We have to go to Ms. Dillwater's house and see what we can find," Dylan suggested, his face determined.

"You mean, break into her house," Sammie responded. "I doubt the back door will be open this time."

"He's right." Rahul had a look of triumph on his face

since going to Ms. Dillwater's house had been his idea from the beginning.

Sammie looked in the direction of the lake. That seemed like the key to her, not looking for clues in a house that the police had already looked in. "But what if the green cloud eye is there again?"

"It hasn't hurt anybody yet," Dylan said.

"Yet." Sammie could remember the whole-body chill she felt both times she'd seen it, a brain freeze times a billion.

But her two friends were set on a course, so she decided to go along. They collected their bikes, finished their freezies, and headed to Poplar Street.

As they came up to the house, the only noise was a breeze ruffling the young spring leaves. There were no neighbors in sight, and no cars coming down the street. They rode past the house once to make sure no one was around.

"Let's approach from behind," Sammie said. The back-yard ended in woods connected to a small city park. So they circled around, rode to the edge of the park, and left their bikes behind a tree in the woods. A few folks wandered the park, but no one seemed to notice three kids doing what kids usually did.

They crept through the woods, more slowly and quietly than they probably needed to be. Getting into Ms. Dillwa-ter's house before had seemed like a natural set of events:

they had come to see her, the back door had been open, and all that. This seemed very different. Last time, getting caught sneaking into the house had seemed like two kids making a slightly bad decision. If they got caught this time, a conqueror from another dimension would not be their only big problem.

When they reached the backyard, all they could hear were a few birds chirping as they circled a tree, and they couldn't see anyone in the neighboring backyards.

"How do we get in?" Rahul said in his too-loud whisper. "The door will be locked for sure."

"My dad got in somehow." The other two looked at Dylan. "Come on, don't you two think my dad broke in? He probably trashed the place looking for clues."

But Dylan's theory didn't completely match what Sammie and Rahul had seen. Furniture had moved rooms. Toothpaste was squirted out. Why would anyone do that?

"Your dad must have seen the green cloud eye too!" Sammie said. "He got spooked by it and ran from the house, leaving the backdoor open. Makes perfect sense. We literally did the same thing."

"But how did he get in?" Rahul asked.

Sammie examined the back of the house. She imagined Dylan's dad had to use the back; the front of the house was on a quiet but open street. Her eyes fell on the three kitchen windows facing the back yard. "There," she said, pointing at the windows. "He probably got in through the windows. They are low enough for an adult to get in."

The boys nodded and followed her in a dash across the yard.

Once they reached the windows, all of them reached up, but Sammie and Dylan could barely reach them, and Rahul couldn't even do that.

"We'll boost you up," Dylan said to Rahul, "and then you can open the window."

"Why me?" Rahul protested. "Why not Sammie?"

Sammie rolled her eyes. "You're the smallest of the three of us."

"I'm more muscle than you think."

"Fine, you're Mr. Incredible," Dylan responded exasperatedly. "Just get ready for a boost."

Sammie and Dylan boosted him up, holding him at their waist. The window was unlocked and came open without much effort. Dylan boosted Sammie next, and Rahul helped pull her in. Getting Dylan in was by far the trickiest part: he had to jump and then the others had to catch his hands and pull him in. On their third attempt, they got him inside.

The small kitchen was much like they'd seen it last time. The drawers were still open, their contents dumped onto the floor. The kitchen chairs were there, turned upright now. The lone lamp shade still sat next to the sink.

"This place is a mess," Dylan muttered quietly, as if he was afraid Ms. Dillwater might hear his assessment of her housekeeping and appear to scold him.

"We should go to the room where we saw green cloud eye appear," Rahul said. "Maybe it was guarding something."

Sammie nodded, but she didn't move, her muscles frozen. She did not want to see that creepy eye again.

"Let's go," Dylan said, the first to move. He'd never seen the green cloud eye and didn't know how scary it was. Rahul had, though, and he followed closely behind. Sammie took a deep breath and followed them into the narrow hall.

The hallway had been cleared of all the rubbish that had been there before; apparently the police had picked up a bit. The light in the bathroom was on, but the room across from it was completely dark. There was no green mist this time, no indication that the trashed house was anything more than a tossed mess.

"I assume we're headed to the creepily dark room on the right," Dylan said.

"Unless you need to pee," Rahul quipped. "The bathroom is on the left."

Dylan pulled out his smart phone and activated his flashlight; Rahul did the same. Sammie wished, for about the billionth time, her parents let her have one of those.

The two boys went first, moving their lights around as they came into the room. Sammie came in but stopped just inside the doorway. The other two stepped in further. She reached over and flicked the light switch.

Both boys jumped as the light came on.

"Don't ever do that again!" Rahul squealed.

"What? Turn on a light switch?" She smiled.

The room was a small office of sorts with only a small, second-hand work desk, a metal chair, and an old cream-colored computer. It was completely clean, not a paper, drawer or item out of place.

The room had been dark because thick, black plastic had been draped around the room's two windows, fixed to the walls with duct tape.

"This house keeps getting creepier," Dylan said.

"Wait until the green eye cloud shows up," Sammie said, stepping past her friends and to the desk.

"Why would a teacher need a room like this?" Rahul asked. "I mean, this is like spy or drug dealer stuff."

"I never liked her," Dylan said.

Sammie stepped up to the desk. The computer was one of those old tower ones with a bunch of slots, a couple she didn't even recognize. And the monitor was big and looked like it weighed a hundred pounds. "What was she doing with a dinosaur computer?"

"Maybe she's a time traveler," Rahul offered. The other two rolled their eyes at him in unison. "What?" he protested. "Like an eggplant from another dimension is any weirder than time travel."

Rahul started looking through the desk drawers and Sammie stepped back and noticed more duct tape in a weird pattern on the left wall. But it was just a weird, jutting shape that covered most of the wall, but nothing else.

"Malsman Lake," Dylan said, stepping up next to her and regarding the blocky shape.

"What?" Sammie asked.

His eyes traced the lines. "The last few weeks, my dad has been looking at maps of the city and county. This is an outline of Malsman Lake, the town of Malsman Lake."

Sammie stepped closer to the wall. She saw dozens of little holes like ones left by little nails or thumb tacks. There was also a few pieces of Scotch tape dotting the shape.

"A map of weird," Sammie muttered.

Rahul stepped over. "A map of weird?"

"Yeah." Sammie traced the taped line with her hand at its edge. "My closet is laid out kind of the same. Ms. Dillwater, or whatever her name really is, was keeping her own List of Mysteries, but in like a map."

"Then where's all the weird stuff?" Dylan asked.

"She took it all down." Sammie stepped back. "Maybe because she knew she was leaving; she took it with her, or someone came in and took it."

"Why would an agent for evil eggplant dude keep a list of weird?" Rahul asked.

"Maybe she was scouting places for the portal thing," Dylan answered. "Remember what the eggplant told Sammie: he'd been trying to find the right place."

"Maybe." Sammie felt like they were missing something important. If Ms. Dillwater had worked for the Eggplant Emperor, how did she get to their dimension before he'd opened a portal? She was also human. Maybe his kind could change shapes, but her being his minion didn't seem quite right.

"Well, the desk is empty." Rahul threw up his hands. "Not even any pens or papers. Nothing but a stupid old computer that looks like it might not even work and a tiny little screwdriver. The computer's not even connected to power or anything, and I can't believe a machine that old would have Wi-Fi built into it."

"Not connected to power?" Sammie turned to the desk and walked up to the computer. "How old do you think Ms. Dillwater is?"

Dylan stepped up next to her. "I dunno. Twenty-five or something. Old."

"That's not that old," Sammie said. Dylan shrugged.

"And she had a smart watch and a smart phone," Rahul said, nodding, starting to get what Sammie was thinking.

"Exactly. Why would someone like that have an old computer like this? Does she seem like she'd be a collector of old stuff?" Sammie walked around the desk and looked at the back of the computer tower. It was metal, not the cream plastic of its front, and it had half-dozen tiny screws.

"Hand me that screwdriver," Sammie said.

Within a few minutes, she'd unscrewed everything, leaving the tiny screws on the desk next to the computer.

"Now what?" Dylan looked at the computer like the green cloud eye might jump out of it.

"We see what's inside," Sammie said and then she pulled the tower apart in a wedge.

A bunch of papers poured out and tumbled out onto the desk and the floor.

"Her List of Mysteries," Rahul said, his eyes wide.

And it was. Most of the same events Sammie had captured in her closet were captured here as they shuffled through the papers. Cynthia Rudding's hair going purple. The disappearance of the St. Mark's church in 1911. The Komodo dragon dog. But there were some Sammie had never heard of. There was an old newspaper article dated March 4, 1975, that told the story of a woman who'd moved out of Malsman Lake after she said she'd been stuck in a dream for six years. And another handwritten note talking about the lake.

I think it's all unraveling at the lake, the note read. *I see the green waves there almost every day. Maybe he's escaping the lake. Or he could be trying to help someone else open a transdimensional portal.*

Sammie showed the handwritten note to the others.

"Who's escaping?" Dylan asked. "I mean, was the eggplant guy trapped in the lake?"

Rahul held up another handwritten note. "This one says

it's all about the lake. Whoever wrote this thought all the recent troubles had to be connected to the lake." The two boys sheepishly looked at her.

"I guess we should have gone to the lake," she replied with a triumphant grin.

"My dad thought Ms. Dillwater was up to something," Dylan said, his eyes firing up. "He wanted to see what she knew."

Sammie looked down at some of the papers, spreading them out on the floor. "But he never found them. He searched the house, but he never found them."

Dylan nodded. "And maybe that green cloud eye saw him or Ms. Dillwater turned him over to her master."

Sammie shook her head. "I don't think she's with him. Look at all this." She spread out her arms. "She was trying to figure it all out, not conquer stuff. She's like us."

"She's not like us," Rahul said. "Maybe she's part of a different evil group."

"Look at this." Dylan held up a printed photo and handed it to Sammie.

It was the picture of an opened closet, Colin's open closet.

"Well having a picture of Colin's closet is pretty good evidence of evilness," Rahul said, wincing. "I mean, she broke into your house."

"But Dylan's dad figured out something weird was

happening at my house," Sammie said back. "I just don't think she's in with the Eggplant Emperor."

"I think she's right," Dylan finally admitted. "This looks like a grown-up version of what Sammie does." He shook his head. "I really thought she was a crazy old witch or a vampire or a monster in disguise."

"But why did she leave all this behind?" Sammie asked, rifling through some papers.

"Excellent question."

All three kids jumped to their feet with the voice. Sheriff Masters stood there, leaning in the doorway. "I thought I told you kids to go home. Pretty sure none of you live here."

CHAPTER 13

"WE WERE JUST--"

But Sheriff Masters cut Rahul off. "I know exactly what you three we're doing." She looked at the scattered papers. "Looks like you three found something we didn't."

"You didn't think of looking inside the computer?" Sammie asked.

"I didn't have a warrant. But now that three criminals have done it, and I can see what's inside..."

Rahul's face went a shade paler. "We're criminals?"

"Relax, Patil, I'm not going to charge you three with anything. But I did tell you to go home, and you three completely disobeyed me. I'm not happy about that." She didn't seem all that disappointed as she knelt down and started going through the papers.

"What is all this?" she asked. But none of them

answered, because it didn't sound like she was asking them. "Who was this woman?"

She started separating the papers, putting scraps and notes into two piles. When she was finished, she took a deep breath and stood up.

"What do you think she was up to?" Sammie asked.

"Do you think she had anything to do with my dad disappearing?" Dylan added.

Sheriff Masters looked at them, then shrugged. "I don't know who she was, and I have no idea if she's connected to your dad or not." She knelt back down, right next to Dylan. "I'm sorry, Dylan, that we can't find your dad. None of this makes sense to me. There's another officer outside. He'll take you to your mom. She's probably worried sick, and I don't think it's fair to make her worry right now."

Dylan looked down at his phone and his eyes widened. "She's texted me six times. I didn't even notice."

Sheriff Masters offered him a soft smile. "She called me right after you three left the station. I figured I knew where you'd go."

"Someone saw us get into the house," Rahul lamented.

The sheriff shook her head. "No, you three were stealthy. But I've been doing this for a while and I recognized the look of three kids who weren't going to give this up." She patted Dylan on the shoulder. "Go on, kid. Your mom needs you right now. Go help her."

He nodded somberly, looked back and Rahul and Sammie, and then left.

Sheriff Masters stood and regarded Rahul. "And you, Patil, should get that satisfied grin off your face and go home before I change my mind about charging you for something."

He nodded like a bobblehead, but he looked over at Sammie.

"She'll be fine," Sheriff Masters said. "I need another word with her. Get going, Patil."

"See ya, Sammie." Rahul offered a half smile.

"Bye, Rahul." Sammie waved at him, wishing he wasn't leaving.

Sheriff Masters kneeled back down by the now ordered papers and started shuffling through them.

"I think she was investigating all the weird stuff," Sammie said, looking over the woman's shoulder.

The sheriff held up a handwritten note. It told the story of a woman who'd reported her son missing. "Have you ever heard of this one?"

Teenage boy goes missing and no one cared, the note read. *It was 1968. Authorities outside of Malsman Lake weren't even contacted until three months after he went missing.*

"No," Sammie said.

Sheriff Masters set the papers down and stood, pacing the room. "When I got here, I thought it would be a nice change. South Chicago is tough to live in, tough to police. I found the file on this kid several years ago. No suspects. No investigation. He'd been adopted a couple years before after he wandered into town. No record of who he was. And then he disappeared, just like he'd appeared, without a trace."

"There's an eggplant in my brother's closet," Sammie spilled out.

Sheriff Masters stopped pacing. "What?"

Sammie took a deep breath and spilled everything, all the details about the Eggplant Emperor, the green cloud eye, and even about her parents being under control of the emperor guy. The sheriff didn't interrupt; she just listened with intense eyes. When Sammie finished, the woman let out a long breath and shook her head.

"You don't believe me," Sammie said, dejected.

"A few weeks ago, I found a house, a silo and a barn missing," the sheriff replied. "But an alien in your brother's closet bent on world domination? Even for Malsman Lake, that seems like a stretch."

"You asked me about my parents. Why? You think something's wrong with them?"

"Maybe." She rested her hands on her broad belt. "I shouldn't tell you any of this." She continued anyway. "Two folks called me because they thought the invitation from your parents was weird. They thought your parents were doing something shady, like one of those pyramid schemes."

"Pyramid what?"

"Doesn't matter. I called your parents, and they acted really weird, and they told me not to come by. That's a strange thing to tell a police officer, especially coming from two law-abiding people who have always been extremely friendly to me."

"So you believe they're being mind-controlled?"

"I don't know Sammie. I don't believe in this supernatural nonsense. This town is filled with the bizarre, but my experience is that there's a rational explanation for things, even for things that don't make sense at first."

Sammie tucked her hands into her pockets. "So you don't believe me."

Sheriff Masters bent down and met Sammie's eyes. "I am your friend, Sammie. If you need me, I will be there. You call me, even if it's to scare away an eggplant creature." She stood back up. "But for now, let's get you home. You leave all this up to me. My team will figure out what's going on."

As Sheriff Masters drove her home, Sammie couldn't fight the feeling that she'd messed everything up, that maybe kids should stay out of these things, that she'd read too many Sideralis books—books that weren't real.

She also knew that they should be in trouble. The sheriff should have, at least, chewed them out and told their parents that they'd not only broken into a home but had disobeyed the sheriff's instructions that they all go home.

Ms. Dillwater's weird map, eventually, pushed aside all those other thoughts. There were so many other things she didn't know about, many of them dangerous. A teenage boy had gone missing when her grandparents had been kids, and she'd never even heard about it. Shouldn't something like that affect a small town? Wasn't stuff like that always remembered? Not in Malsman Lake. In Malsman Lake, nothing seemed to matter. Which made it the perfect place to launch an invasion from a different dimension.

When they pulled into Sammie's driveway, she saw her parents standing on the porch, as if they'd been waiting for them to come.

"Did you call my parents?" Sammie asked, worried that the trouble she thought she'd avoided was coming her way.

"I didn't call them." The sheriff's voice wavered worriedly, which only made Sammie more nervous. As she put the car in park, Sheriff Masters turned in her seat and faced Sammie, her face stern through the thick plastic separating them. "Listen to me, Sammie: if you need me, call me. No matter what. Deal?"

Sammie nodded, but she couldn't even say yes through the knot growing in her belly.

Sammie slinked from the car and collected her bike from the trunk, walking it up slowly toward the porch.

Her parents waved at Sheriff Masters as she backed away, their smiles too wide, their eyes too happy, like a couple in a movie saying goodbye to a dear relative.

And as soon as the sheriff's vehicle disappeared from view, their faces turned to the couple about to ship off their oldest daughter to boarding school.

"Get inside," Dad said.

"Up to your room," Mom said.

Sammie took a deep breath and tried not to cry. What could even Sheriff Masters do against an alien emperor from another dimension?

Sammie did as she was told, putting her bike away and walking up the stairs, each step feeling like a hundred.

"Colin?" she called.

"He's downstairs watching the television," Dad said behind her.

"He's fine," Mom said.

"We need to talk with you," Dad said, his tone lacking all of its usual warmth.

"In your room, Samantha," Mom said, her voice lacking the bite it usually had when she was angry.

Sammie stepped into her room, her parents right behind. Her room was not messy. It had been cleaned, all the clothes were off the floor, and the papers were organized on her desk. Even the closet was tidy.

The closet was open, filled with her clothes again like it had been when she was little, and all her weird stuff was gone.

CHAPTER 14

SHE TURNED ON HER PARENTS. "Where is my List of Mysteries?"

"Gone," Mom said.

"In the garbage," Dad added.

She felt panic rise from her stomach into her chest. "But that's my stuff."

"Silly stuff," Dad said.

"Ridiculous stuff," Mom echoed.

"Stop talking like that!" Sammie screamed. "That is not how you talk! My mother and father don't talk like that! Eggplant Emperor: I know you're in there! Leave my parents alone, you monster."

Sammie's parents exchanged a blank look, and then looked back at her.

"Eggplant Emperor?" Dad questioned.

"More silly stuff," Mom said.

"You are to stay in your room," Dad commanded, stepping halfway out of the room.

"Until the dinner hour," Mom instructed.

"And no more friends for a few days," Dad said, his face trying on a too-deep frown that looked like Colin when he didn't get his way.

"No Rahul Patil, no Dylan Schumacher," Mom said, her eyebrows tight in a silly-looking scowl.

Sammie wanted to scream, wanted to yell at them. But what would that do? She wasn't talking to Randy and Shannon Stadler; she was talking to Tal-Shah-Whatever-His-Name and he wasn't going to listen.

So as her parents closed the door to her room, she fell onto her bed and cried.

━━━

At dinner, her parents seemed normal, but Sammie wasn't sure if they were back for a moment or if Eggplant Emperor was just getting better at pretending to be human.

After cleaning up dinner as a family, her parents joking, her brother whining, it seemed normal. But Sammie didn't feel like normal. Worry held her so tight that breathing seemed to hurt.

Dad headed to the garage to work on something, and Mom went to give Colin a bath. Sammie went to her room to think.

She sat on her bed staring at her closet. Instead of her List of Mysteries, it looked like the closet of any 11-year-old girl: a few dresses for Sunday, followed by t-shirts and sweatshirts. No sticky notes, no old newspaper articles, no internet printouts. Looking at it made her feel like she'd been punched in the gut.

Should she call Sheriff Masters? And tell her what? That her parents had cleaned her room and reorganized her closet? That hardly seemed like an emergency requiring the police. But the sheriff had been worried. Even if she didn't believe in other dimensions, Sheriff Masters knew something was wrong.

She thought about heading to Rahul's house. But how would she explain showing up after dark on a Saturday night? Lata would call Sammie's mom, and she was sure the eggplant would order her home.

And Dylan. He was sitting in a hotel room with his mother and sisters. She'd seen the drive in his eyes. No matter what Sheriff Masters said, he wasn't going to just sit and wait for the police to find his dad. He would keep looking, maybe for the rest of his life. And Sammie had promised that she would help.

Dylan. His idea had been to go into Colin's room and sit there until the Eggplant Emperor showed himself. Well, that seemed like the only idea left.

Sammie stood up, the motion harder than she thought it would be. The Eggplant Emperor controlled her parents and had possibly caused Ms. Dillwater and Mr. Schumacher to disappear. What exactly would she say or do in the face of that? She was a kid, and he ruled eighty-four dimensions; she didn't even get to decide her own bedtime.

But she couldn't just sit here and watch the evil vegetable tear Malsman Lake apart. Maybe it was a weird town, but Malsman Lake was her home.

She walked across her room, opened the door and crossed the hall.

Colin's room had also been cleaned, all the toys organized against the walls, his little toddler bed made with the comforter folded nicely at its foot. It seemed perfect, too perfect to be normal, especially for the Stadler house.

Sammie faced the closet. The door was closed tight, the white, paneled wood looking at her like a giant stone face. That thought did not help her nervousness.

Sammie reached out and threw the closet open.

Like it had that day, the contents of Colin's closet were gone, replaced by a swirling space too large to fit in a small closet. The green sky pulsed and some wisps of green mist escaped and curled around her feet.

And in the center was the Eggplant Emperor in all his purple-bodied, green-headed, spaghetti-limbed creepiness.

"Hello once more, Samantha Stadler," called the same, mouthless voice she'd heard weeks before.

"Hello, Eggplant Emperor."

"My name is Tal-Shah-Farneree Tublat," he spoke, the

voice sending a chill up Sammie's back. "You should show more respect for your future leader."

A feeling pounded in her brain. She should run. She should close the closet and run far away. She couldn't do anything against Tal-Shah-Farneree Tublat, master of eighty-four dimensions. She couldn't fight this.

But then she thought of her parents, their minds spoiled by Tublat. She thought of Dylan, his family ripped apart by this thing. And she thought of her town, most of it unaware of the danger that was coming.

No. Even if she was scared, she wouldn't run away, she wouldn't give in. She didn't know how, but she knew that she would fight.

"You're not my future leader," she said, pulling her hands into fists at her side. "You're more likely to get turned into an appetizer."

It laughed. "You are brave, Samantha Stadler. I could use someone like you in my army. You know this dimension in ways my kind never will, its customs, its oddities. Join me, offspring, and you shall be a queen, a master."

"Leave my family alone," she growled.

Tublat's eggplant body twisted. "I cannot do that. You have the unfortunate circumstance of living where my portal worked. It is not personal. And the forces that used to protect this place also left its inhabitants weak-minded."

Forces that protected the place? Did he mean her world or Malsman Lake?

"But it doesn't matter," it said, laughing a little. "Those forces are gone, forgotten or destroyed. It does not matter, Samantha Stadler. At my side, you will be a queen. Against me, you will be a slave."

"Why haven't you made me your slave then? Doesn't seem to work with me or my brother."

Its body shifted again. "Hmm. I cannot explain it. But your resistance is like a calraqqi fighting a binder-beast."

"I don't know what those things are, you smelly eggplant. Purple is not a good color for you, and I don't think I can eat spaghetti ever again after watching your arms wave like that."

"Your meaningless insults are, well, meaningless. After tomorrow night, I will have your little settlement under my control. And once that is complete, I can move behind this tiny place. Soon, I will have an eighty-fifth dimension in my control, and there's nothing a small offspring like you can do. Your people will tremble before the greatness of the undefeatable--"

Sammie reached across and slammed the door shut. "Oh, shut up, Eggplant. There's no way I'm going to let that happen."

Sammie waited for a few moments for the closet door to fly open or for the green cloud eye to emerge. But nothing happened. The green mist evaporated. She reached out and eased the closet open a sliver and revealed nothing but Colin's normal closet.

Sammie didn't know how she was going to stop Tublat, but she wasn't going to just sit and let his plan take shape. If the party the next night was the first key to all of this, then she would make sure that it was the worst Eggplant Emperor party in the history of all of his dimensions.

CHAPTER 15

SAMMIE AWOKE ON SUNDAY MORNING, assuming she'd hear the family preparing for church. But the house, despite the sun rising above the horizon, was eerily silent. No sounds of her father working in his shop or mother's clicks at her keyboard. And no Colin either.

She went downstairs to find a note on counter, one written in her mom's usual flowing handwriting.

You've seemed very tired lately, so we let you sleep. Took Colin to breakfast. See you soon.

If not for the crazy events of the past few weeks, this would have seemed normal. They occasionally skipped church and went to breakfast, and Mom was always talking about how adolescents needed tons of sleep. But Sammie's mind turned to how this breakfast could work in Eggplant Emperor's favor.

But no, that was Mom's handwriting and Mom's voice

in the note. He didn't control them all the time, just sometimes. Her parents were still in there; she just needed to figure how to get them all the way free.

She scribbled a note saying she was going for a bike ride and would be back soon, and then she ate a quick peanut butter and jelly sandwich before leaving.

She biked at full speed to Rahul's house, and as she turned off the street and onto his longish driveway, she saw Rahul and Dylan sitting on the porch. Both of them jumped to their feet when they saw her.

"You escaped!" Rahul exclaimed. "I've been so worried. You really need a phone."

"I know," she said, "I know. So much has happened."

She filled them in on her parents weirdness when she got home and her conversation with the Eggplant Emperor.

"They're going to mind mite all the adults in town," Dylan muttered, "at least the ones coming to the party."

Sammie nodded. "Yeah. And then he can spread, maybe like a virus or something."

"Sheriff Masters might help us," Rahul said. "I mean, it seems like she partly believes."

Sammie shook her head. "No, she is searching for a rational explanation for all of this. But there isn't one. We're talking about a freaking eggplant creature from another dimension and mind control. She probably thinks its drugs or that my parents have started a cult or something."

"Your parents starting a cult would be less scary," Rahul said, shivering despite a jacket and warm spring air.

"So what now?" Dylan asked.

"The lake." Sammie picked up her bike. "Ms. Dillwater, or whatever her name really is, believed that something at the lake was the key to all this. We need to check it out."

This time, neither boy offered any objection. Rahul grabbed two bikes from his garage, one that was a little too big for Dylan but he managed anyway. They sped away for the lake.

Sammie thought about taking the long way to the lake. The direct route took the road right by Dylan's old house, but they needed to be quick. The party was hours away, and if whatever they found at the lake could help stop what was coming, they needed to make it happen fast.

The group slowed and then stopped as they came by Dylan's house. Unlike a few weeks before, the trees now had buds and some leaves, blocking their view a little. A deep frown crossed Dylan's face.

"Do you think there's any chance we can get my house back?" he asked.

"I don't know," Sammie said and Rahul shrugged.

"I had a signed copy of Danger in the Stars," Dylan said, his eyes fixed on the missing house. "My dad was on a business trip in Chicago and went to a signing with Makenzie Greenwood."

"Your dad met Makenzie Greenwood?" Sammie

couldn't control her enthusiasm despite the somberness of the moment. Makenzie Greenwood was the author of the Sideralis Academy series. If the main character, Andromeda Rodriguez, was Sammie's fictional hero, then Makenzie Greenwood was her real-life hero.

Sammie's excitement made Dylan smile. "Yeah. Said she was super nice, despite the thousand people packed in this bookstore all trying to get books signed. I kept that book right by my bed." He didn't cry, but he looked darn close.

"Let's get to the lake and figure this all out." Sammie took a deep breath. "I'm not sure we can set all this right, Dylan, but, by the stars, we're going to try."

He smiled again at the use of the phrase "by the stars." It was the catch phrase of Ye-Jun Kim, the principal of Sideralis Academy.

"Then, by the stars, let's get to the lake."

The lake was quiet. Despite the warm sun and early spring, the water would still be frigid; the lake had been frozen not that long ago. In a few months it would be filled with canoes and swimmers on the north shore, but now it was quiet. And covered in green mist.

"Everyone else is seeing the green stuff, right?" Dylan's eyes were wide and his mouth stayed open a little even after his question.

"Ten-four," Rahul said.

"Ten what?" Dylan looked over at him.

"It's walkie-talkie for yes."

"We're not using walkie-talkies, dude."

Like most of the times Sammie had seen the green mist, it held steady like a fog hovering in place, but even more so. It didn't flinch with the wind, was not disturbed by the ripples on the lake's surface. It just hung there.

"If my parents were here, they wouldn't see it," Sammie said. Her parents; she needed to help her parents.

"Now what?" Rahul said, turning to look at her.

What to do now? They hadn't spent enough time with Ms. Dillwater's stuff to understand why she thought the lake was the key to all of this. Her note had mentioned someone escaping or trying to open a portal.

"Do you thinks Ms. Dillwater thought Eggplant Emperor was using the lake?" she asked.

"I dunno," Rahul said. "Nothing we saw mentioned anything like eggplant dude."

"So she was talking about someone else?" Dylan offered.

Sammie looked out over the lake. She's been on this shore many times. There were a half-dozen 'No Swimming' signs. Swimming was only allowed on the northern shore.

"Why can't you swim on this side?" Sammie asked.

"Safety, I bet," Dylan said, regarding one of the warning signs.

"But why is it safer?" She stepped back farther up the

bank to get a better view of the north shore. "There's no green mist up there by the swimming place."

Rahul dropped his bike and joined her on the embankment. "Holy crap. Is there ever green mist over there?"

"I don't know," Sammie responded. "I'd never thought to think like that. But it covers the east and the south, the western shore is clear too. It doesn't cover all the lake."

Dylan joined them. "Maybe it's the light or something."

Sammie squinted. "Maybe. We'd have to bike around there to get a better look."

"Circling the lake will take us all day," Rahul said. "We don't have that much time. 'It's all unraveling at the lake.' What did the pretend Ms. Dillwater mean by that?"

"There's only one way to find out." Sammie sat down on the packed dirt and started taking off her shoes.

"What are you doing?" Rahul demanded.

"What does it look like? I'm going for a swim."

"But the signs say no swimming," Rahul responded.

She rolled her eyes. "Your big idea was for us to break into a house. I'm pretty sure this is not as serious."

Dylan sat down and started talking off his shoes. "Would have brought my suit if I'd known we were swimming."

"Do you know how cold that water is going to be?" Rahul said. "It's probably like forty-something degrees. That's like hypothermia type water."

Sammie looked at her best friend. He was breathing

heavy, even though they'd stopped biking minutes ago. He was moving his fingers nervously along the edge of his t-shirt.

"What's wrong, Rahul?"

"We should call Sheriff Masters or something."

"And tell her what?" Dylan stood and set his socks and shoes next to his borrowed bike. "That there's a mist on the lake? Or that we're trying to stop an alien invasion? Sammie already tried that; the sheriff isn't going to help us."

"But what if you're dad figured it out too?" Rahul said, his voice higher than usual. "And the pretend Ms. Dillwater. If they both thought it was lake, and then swam into it. Now they're both gone."

Sammie stood facing her friend. He was nearly shaking, and she knew that fear; it had been with her too.

"My parents are under mind control," Sammie said, taking Rahul's arm. "Dylan's dad is gone. Tublat-what's-his-worship is going to take over Malsman Lake tonight. We have to do something, and this is the best idea we've got, even if it stinks."

He looked down, considering. "Maybe we need to think harder about other ideas."

"Rahul." He looked into her eyes. "What would Joe Mauer do?"

He offered a half smile. "Joe Mauer is a baseball player, not a superhero."

"Fine. But what would he do?"

Rahul looked at the lake. "He'd probably go in and try and figure this out." He looked back at her. "That's a pretty dirty trick, Sammie."

She smiled. "I figured that my usual 'What would Andromeda Rodriguez do?' speech wouldn't work on you."

Rahul sat down and took off his shoes and then his socks, sticking the Twins-themed socks into his shoes.

The three of them stood on the shore, their bare toes nearly at the edge of the water.

"How deep are we going to go?" Dylan said, his voice sounding nearly as nervous as Rahul.

"We should stay where we can stand," Sammie suggested. "Rahul's not a great swimmer."

He scoffed. "I'm a fish compared to you."

"Let's do it together," Sammie said. "On three, we'll talk one step into the water. One, two, three."

They stepped into the water, submerging both their feet.

Dylan squealed. "Holy crap, the water is freezing."

"I told you," Rahul reminded him.

But nothing else happened. It was just cold water on their feet.

"A few more steps, then," Sammie said.

They took a few more slow steps together. The icy water sent a powerful shiver across Sammie's body and it stopped her breath for a moment.

"I'll never feel my feet again," Rahul complained.

"Four more steps." Sammie led as they stepped up into their waist.

The chill was almost crippling at this point, Sammie's legs screaming that she needed to get out. But she couldn't.

"Four more steps," she repeated, and they moved together again.

As they stopped, the water at their chests, the still green mists began to move, swirling slowly around them. Some of it coalesced into a small cloud, and a bright green slit turned into a bright eye. Below it, the mists swirled faster and faster, forming a funnel cloud around them, though the air did not stir.

"This was a very bad idea," Rahul said, his teeth chattering as he spoke.

Sammie felt her feet sinking, like she'd stepped into deep mud. She raised her hands, trying to keep her balance. Out of the corner of her eye, she saw Dylan do the same.

Then the green funnel cloud tightened around them, and she was sucked into the lake, her vision filled with nothing but bright green light.

CHAPTER 16

SAMMIE HELD her breath as long as she could, feeling the cold water all around her. But then she couldn't wait any longer. She opened her mouth when her body wouldn't let her keep it closed any longer.

But no water rushed in, only really cold air. She gasped, not sure how she was breathing.

She looked left and right, trying to see if Rahul and Dylan had joined her. But all she could see was green light. She felt like she was in one of the free fall rides, except it was going too long. She waved her arms, as if that might slow her fall, but it did nothing.

A few moments later, she felt herself slowing. And then she landed.

The bright swirling cloud pulled away, much like it had first begun. As it pulled away, it revealed Rahul at her left and Dylan on her right. And then, standing in front of them, was another person. Not an eggplant, or a giant green eye, but a person.

He looked like a teenager torn from an old movie. He wore a burgundy letterman's jacket with the letters 'ML' marked in gold above his left breast. His skin glowed with a little of the green light, as did his eyes, like a cat in the night. His hair was poofy and his tight jeans were rolled up at the ankles.

"Welcome to the bottom of the lake," the young man said. "I wish I had drinks or something to offer, but I'm kind of limited down here."

"Where are we?" Dylan croaked, his voice echoing. "Where is my dad?"

"Dude," the young man said, showing his hands. "Not polite to ask questions out of order. Don't you want to know where you are first?"

"You already told us we were at the bottom of the lake," Sammie said. She looked up to see a dome of green light above them.

"And you're not at all curious about how you're breathing at the bottom of the lake?"

"Who are you?" Rahul breathed.

"We're getting closer to the right order, daddy-o." He walked toward them and stopped when they all took a step back. "Easy, cats. I'm not going to hurt you. I let you come down here because we need to talk. You have questions, and I have all the right answers, but we've got to do this in the right order. Do you feel me?"

"Are you working with the Eggplant Emperor, Tublat?" Sammie asked.

The young man's face flickered, the light fading some. "Well, that's way out of order, Sammie, but I'll answer that one straight up. I wouldn't have anything to do with that two-bit wanna-be fat cat, not for all the gold in Fort Knox. I've tried to talk him out of his stupid plan, but he's thicker than brick wall."

He began pacing back and forth, pivoting on his Chuck Taylor sneakers. "Now, we just need to ask things in the right order."

"How come we can breathe down here?" Sammie asked.

"Smart girl." He stopped pacing and smiled at her. "The obvious brains of your little gang." He looked at Rahul. "You're the fire." And then at Dylan. "And, well, I'm not sure what you're bringing. Pretty sure these two could have done all this on their own." He looked back at Sammie. "We can breathe down here because I brought you into my little jail cell."

Rahul looked around. "Jail cell?"

"Yeah." He waved around the green dome with his arms. "Not much of a home, but the fuzz are the fuzz, and I'm here."

"The fuzz?" Dylan questioned.

"Yeah. Flatfoots. The man. You know. The police, or at

least my version of them. They call themself the Dimensionera." He frowned at the name. "I call them no-good, filthy fat cats."

The three kids looked at one another.

The young man regarded them. "Don't the cool kids talk like this anymore?"

"I'm not sure anyone talked like that ever," Rahul replied, "except for maybe in the movies."

The young man smiled. "Well, I'm kinda stuck in a lot of ways."

"Why did those Dimensionera people put you here?" Sammie asked.

"Ding!" The young man jumped with excitement. "That's the right next question. Very good, Sammie Stadler." He sat down on a chair that hadn't been there a moment before. Chairs also appeared right behind each of the kids. "Have a seat, kiddos."

They exchanged another look but all sat.

"The Dimensionera are like cops, but across dimensions. The ones based here in your dimension are the worst, like feds mixed with the reds." He waited for a reaction, but after they didn't give any, he threw his hands into the air. "The reds? The commies? The Soviets? Gosh, don't they teach history in your little school?

"Anyway, they get you for the smallest infractions. I mean, a cool guy like me is just minding his own business, and the next thing you know I'm in a prison at the bottom of a stinking lake. How not cool is that?"

"What did you do?" Dylan asked.

He crossed his legs and looked at Dylan. "A minor infraction, son."

"Like you stole a street sign or like you tried to conquer our dimension?" Rahul asked.

The young man smiled like a cat right before it pounced on a mouse. "Much closer to street sign theft than dimension conquering."

"Who are you?" Sammie asked.

He stood and clapped his hands, excited. "Man, Sammie, I knew you were smart, but to ask all these questions in the right order? Dang, kid, you're about as hip as can be."

"How do you know about Sammie?" Rahul asked.

The young man's excitement faded and he frowned at Rahul. "You might be the biggest square in town. That is not the right order, but since you and the jock can't seem to keep up, I'll oblige you."

He faced them, standing, with his hands raised above his head like he was calling a touchdown. Some of the swirling mist from the domed walls coalesced above his head in a little cloud. A green slit appeared, and the now familiar green cloud eye returned.

"You're with him," Sammie said. "That's the eye that's been following me. That's Tublat's eye!"

The young man lowered his hands and the green cloud eye dissipated. "And I thought you were the smart one. No, that's my eye. That eggplant clown couldn't conjure something like that if his fat life depended on it."

"So you've been watching us," Rahul said.

"Ding! Ding!" He pointed at Rahul. "The comic relief provides some real value to the conversation."

"Comic relief?" Rahul exclaimed. "You think I'm funny?" He smiled and nodded.

"But back to the right question," the young man continued. "You can call me the Cool Guy."

"The Cool Guy?" Dylan looked at him with a skeptical look. "By calling yourself cool, doesn't that make you not cool?"

The Cool Guy nearly growled at Dylan. "I'd thought the other popular boy would be sympathetic to my plight as the coolest wolf in the pack." He sat back down in his chair. "I come from another dimension. I'm not human, though I can take form to look like you ankle biters."

"Ankle biters?" they all asked together.

"Seriously, you three are starting to bug. Ankle biters. Kids. Anyway, I came here hundreds of years ago to cruise for a while. I found that this was my favorite dimension, so I stayed." He looked up at the green dome. "I didn't realize this was going to become my permanent home."

"This is a nice story and all," Sammie said, losing her patience with Cool Guy, "but we came here looking for a way to stop Tublat from taking over our dimension and ruining our lives. Can you help with that?"

Cool Guy leaned forward in his chair, his elbow on his knees, his eyes lighting with excitement, wearing a cat-about-to-pounce smile. "That's the right question, Sammie. Yes, I can help you. I can trap that germ right here in the lake. But I need a solid from you curtain climbers."

"Curtain climbers?" Dylan asked.

"What do you want from us?" Sammie said, ignoring the weird phrases.

"Freedom." He sat back in his chair, his expression casual again. "I don't want dough, I don't want a title to a cherry ride, I just want out."

Sammie sighed. "We don't even know how to stop Tublat. How can we ever get you out?"

He smiled his cat-grin again. "You might not, not right away. If we capture Tublat, then the Dimensionera will take notice of you. And, that's all I really need. Just promise me you'll help me get out when the time comes." He waved around the dome again. "I can be patient. I've been here a long time. So do we have a deal?"

The three friends exchanged a glance.

"What about my dad?" Dylan asked.

Cool Guy frowned, his face serious for the first time. "Tublat, that disgusting worm, took him because your dad's curiosity was getting to be too much. If we get Tublat down here, I will make him give your dad back."

"I'm in," Dylan replied quickly.

But Sammie wasn't so sure. Who was Cool Guy? If these Dimensionera police people had put him at the bottom of the lake, it was likely because he was dangerous. And he'd been complimenting them all, just like adults did before they asked you to do something like clean a toilet. This guy wasn't being honest with them. He might even be worse than Eggplant Emperor.

She looked at Rahul and he looked back, nodding, his expression telling her what she already knew: they didn't have much choice. They only had a few hours to stop Tublat before he controlled Malsman Lake and then the world.

Sammie looked back at Cool Guy. "You have a deal."

He stood up and clapped his hands. "Then we should get you kiddos back to the shore. Just get that purple villain here at the lake, and I will do the rest."

And without another word, the mist swirled around them again, and Cool Guy faded as the feeling of a fast-moving elevator churned Sammie's stomach.

CHAPTER 17

STANDING ON THE RIVERBANK, somehow completely dry, Sammie felt like they could do this. They had a plan now, maybe not an easy plan, but better than nothing. They just had to get Eggplant Emperor down to the lake somehow and this weird Cool Guy would trap him. She stood between her two friends and felt like cheering.

"Do you think we can trust that guy?" Dylan asked, brushing his clothes like he was trying to dry them but finding them dry already.

"Definitely not," Rahul said, his face locked in amazement. "Who talks like that?"

"We don't have to completely trust him," Sammie said, feeling braver and calmer then she had in days. "We just need to get Eggplant Emperor down here tonight and get him trapped."

"And get my dad back," Dylan growled.

"So what's next?" Rahul looked at them both.

"We get ready to wreck that stupid party."

They sped away from the lake on their bikes and decided to meet again in another hour at Rahul's house. Rahul and Dylan would prepare some distractions and Sammie would scout out her house for what was going on.

As Sammie pulled into her driveway, her bright feeling sank into the pit of her stomach. Her parents stood on the porch again, just as they had when Sheriff Masters had dropped her off. But she recognized those expressions. It wasn't the blank mind-controlled look, but anger like she'd seen only once or twice in her life, and never directed at her.

"Where have you been?" her mother growled as Sammie pulled up. "We've been worried sick. That note said you were going on a bike ride. You've been gone for hours!"

"We nearly called Sheriff Masters," her dad said, his tone his normal deep voice, but cold with anger.

Were these the words of her parents, or had Tublat learned to better control them to make them seem normal? He'd proven terrible at making them seem normal, so this was probably the real deal. Part of her was happy to hear their true voices, but it would have been better if they hadn't been so angry.

"I thought with your party preparations, you wouldn't--"

"I'm not particularly interested in your excuses, Samantha." Her mother barked out her name. "Put that bike away, and not on the lawn. Now."

Sammie nodded and hurried to put her bike in the garage. She went in through that door and found her parents standing in the kitchen.

But their faces had changed. Gone were the lines of anger, Mom's quivering eyebrow and gathered lips. Instead they wore nearly comedic expressions of anger, Mom's eyebrows drawn too close, and Dad shaking his head like it was stuck on a swivel.

"Child of ours, you are in trouble," her mother said, the bite from before replaced by a plastic monotone.

"Trouble, trouble, trouble," he father repeated, his head still shaking back and forth.

Sammie felt like she was going to puke. This return to strangeness proved he Tublat hadn't become a better actor. But he had been smart. Her parents had been legitimately angry, so he let them free just long enough to draw her into the house. And it had worked.

"Stop the puppet show, Eggplant," Sammie scowled. "I know it's you now. We don't need to pretend."

At the same moment, the fake angry faces on both parents faded into the same creepy grin.

"You are quite smart, Samantha Stadler," her mother said.

"Just not smart enough," her father intoned.

She didn't know what to say to him, not wanting to give

anything away about their plans. So she decided to bluff. "Your plan is going to fail, and we're going to make a great vegetarian lasagna out of you. The Dimensionera have been made aware and so have the police."

For a brief moment, both faces showed mild concern, but the wicked grin came back just as fast. "Your plan is the one that shall fail," both parents spoke at once. Sammie had thought the alternating speech had been creepy; speaking together was even worse. "We chased off the Dimensionera easily enough; they are shadows of their old selves. And your dimension's authorities? They won't believe you, and they cannot stop my army. Tonight we start conquering this dimension!"

Sammie turned to run, hoping she could get to the garage door faster than they could. But her mother darted around her blocking the way, and her father picked her up, slinging Sammie over his broad shoulder.

She considered resisting, considered hitting and kicking. But she didn't want to hurt her dad, and he was too strong anyway. He'd been a football player in high school and college and was still built like one.

"No, no, no," her father said.

"We can't have you running off," Mom added.

"I thought my plan was destined to fail," Sammie replied as her dad carried her upstairs, her mom trailing behind them.

"Caution is wise," her mother said.

"Oh so wise," her father echoed.

They entered her room and her father dumped her onto her bed with a thud.

"You will not leave this room," her father said.

"Not until the conquest is complete," her mother added.

Like you can stop me, Sammie thought to herself, folding her arms across her chest.

As if hearing her thoughts, their eyes drifted to the room's one window. Sammie had a fire escape ladder under her bed, but she saw that it wouldn't matter. Brackets and screws had been installed at each joint; the window was not going to be an option. Tublat had had her parents screw her window shut!

Panic filled her as her parents backed out of the room.

The door closed followed by a click. Installed at the top of the door was a dead bolt, the paint around it worn off and some of the wood jagged.

"No!" she screamed, running at the door.

She heard their footsteps move away in eerie synchronicity. As soon as they faded down the stairs, she tried the door, but it did not budge even a smidge. She turned to the window, but the result was the same. The window was shut like he'd used cement. Maybe she could break out the glass and the frames, but that would be hard. She knelt to look beneath her bed, and sure enough, the fire escape ladder was gone. Even if she managed to bust the window, she'd have to jump from the second story.

She sat down on her bed and buried her head in her hands. Coming back to scout the house had been a silly mistake. And now her friends had no way of knowing what happened to her. They had decided that Rahul and Dylan could not call the Stadler house, as that would tip Tublat off that something was up. Maybe when they came to disrupt the party, assuming her disappearance wouldn't scare them off their plan, maybe she could signal them and get some help.

Just as she was about to flop down onto her bed, a sound kept her upright. It was the distant ringing of a cell phone, but not the ring of either of her parents. And as she stood, she realized it wasn't that distant. She stepped toward her dresser and put her ear close. The dresser shook a little from the buzzing inside it.

She opened the second drawer, and the ringing got louder. She rummaged through her socks and found a small, old-fashioned flip phone at the bottom of the drawer. The small screen said 'Rahul' on it.

She wasn't even sure how to answer it; she'd never used a phone like this and couldn't find an 'answer' button or icon. So she flipped it open and held it to her ear.

"Hello?"

"Oh, thank the gods," Rahul's voice spoke on the other end. "I wasn't sure this was going to work."

Rahul would have appreciated the stunned expression she was certain she wore on her face. "How is there a cell phone in my room?" She tried to keep her voice down just in case her mind mite parents were close by.

"I know you said no burner phones, but I ignored you," he replied.

"You bought a phone?"

"Of course not. This is Dad's old phone. The fossil only got a smart phone six months ago. He kept this one and pays for service because he says he doesn't trust his fancy phone. So it just sits in a drawer. I dropped it in your socks last time I was there. Just really glad I didn't open the underwear drawer by mistake; that would have been mighty embarrassing."

"You what?"

"I know, you said no spy stuff, but I needed to make sure I could get a hold of you. Sorry."

If he'd been close enough, she would have hugged him.

"After you peeled off," Rahul continued, "Dylan said sending you back to the house was maybe not smart, especially alone. So he went after you. Can you stop being so fast on a bike? He got to your house just in time to see your parents chewing you out."

Sammie told Rahul about her parents and her improvised jail.

"I'm really beginning to hate eggplant dude," Rahul said when she was done.

"Me too. What's the plan now?"

"We disrupt the party in a big way." A smile rang in his voice.

"How? We're not even sure what the party plans are."

"Doesn't matter. As soon as Dylan gets back, we're on our way over. He went to their storage unit to get one of those microphone horn things and an axe, and I've been gathering fireworks from--"

"Don't come rescue me."

The line went silent, almost like the call had dropped. "Sammie, what are you talking about? We need to come--"

"Don't come rescue me," she repeated.

Another pause. "When did we first meet?"

"What? Rahul, we don't have time--"

"I need to know you're not under his power now too."

"Rahul," she cried exasperated, "if eggplant had me, wouldn't I want to lure you into a trap or something? Not keep you away?"

"How am I supposed to understand something that has eggplant for brains? So answer the question: how'd we meet?"

She remembered meeting Rahul like it was yesterday. It had changed everything. The Patil family had moved in just before the start of first grade. During the second week, she'd been out playing with a couple of girls during recess. She'd been friends with some of them, though they weren't close. She'd already become obsessed with the Sideralis Academy and wanted to play that during recess, but the other girls had wanted to play tag with a group of boys. So Sammie had wandered off, looking for someone else to play with.

She found Rahul sitting by himself. The brown boy was so different than anyone else at Malsman Lake Elementary. He'd been trying to join a game of football, but the boys had refused to let him join, saying something cruel about playing American football and not whatever they played in India.

Sammie had approached him and asked him if they wanted to play. Rahul had agreed. She played as Andromeda Rodriguez, and he pretended to be a space agent named Brian Dozier, the name of some Twins player. It had worked. With Sammie and Rahul, it had always worked.

So she told him the story as she remembered it.

"Ok, that's good," he said when she'd finished, "but what if he's accessed your memories?"

"Oh come on, Rahul! It's me! Don't be a ninny!"

"Ok, ok. That is definitely Sammie. So why shouldn't we come bust you out?"

"Tublat is worried I might know something. I told him I had alerted the Dimensionera, whoever they are. He looked a little worried and locked me away."

"I get it. Good plan. Make him think he's taken you out of the picture."

"So what's this about fireworks?"

Rahul told of their plan. They'd use the megaphone,

fireworks, and bright flashlights to get all the guests distracted and hopefully out of the house.

"If they're under its control," Rahul finished, "then they might come to shut us up. If they aren't yet, I can't imagine a bunch of adults won't come out to see what all the commotion's about. And while we make all the noise, one of us will come get you out."

Sammie smiled. "And then I become the bait and we draw him to the lake!"

"What?"

"Eggplant thinks I know something, thinks I'm a danger. When you bust me out, we go for the lake and then trap him."

"Yeah," Rahul said. "A couple years stuck with that Cool Guy will be sufficient punishment, I think."

"Call me back before you launch your distraction," she said. "Until then, I'll be the perfect prisoner."

CHAPTER 18

THE HOURS SAMMIE spent waiting for the party were harder than she had imagined they would be. She kept thinking about how the plan could go wrong, about whether the Cool Guy was really just an agent of the Eggplant Emperor or a fraud who couldn't help them.

And her thoughts kept landing on her family. Her parents were under Tublat's control. And where was Colin? Had they locked him in his bedroom as well? In all the planning to protect their dimension, she'd forgotten to worry about protecting her little brother, and that made her feel terrible. What kind of big sister didn't look out for her little brother, even if he was annoying most of the time?

Rahul texted Sammie just before their disruptions started, but she wouldn't have needed it. She could hear the people below her in the family room and kitchen, the buzz of conversation coming through the floor like a gathering of insects below her. And then she heard the fireworks.

The fireworks started small, just a few pops, surely heard by the adults, but likely dismissed as the actions of bored teenagers in a small town. But then they grew more frequent, louder, and closer. A few bright flashes of color lit the darkness outside the window, red and gold sparks against the blackness of the night and the twinkling of the stars.

All at once, the conversation below stopped, as if Sammie had been watching a movie and paused it. But then the conversation began again, like it hadn't just spontaneously stopped.

Sammie's phone rang.

"It's not working," Rahul said on the other line. "They came to the windows and looked out, but they aren't leaving."

"Time for phase two," Sammie commanded.

She wouldn't be able to see this part coming from the front of the house, but she would hear it. Rahul and Dylan were going to position the two super bright flashlights in the front yard and shine them into the Stadler house. This would get Tublat's attention.

The conversation below again stopped, the silence as sudden turning off a light.

"This is the police," came a loud voice from outside. It was Rahul, but he was doing a good job of making his kid voice sound deeper and more serious. "This party violates lots of codes and stuff. We need everyone to come out. Come out now or...well, we'll start shooting."

We'll start shooting? Those were not the words they had rehearsed. If the adults weren't under the control of the Eggplant Emperor, they'd know for certain that it wasn't Sheriff Masters and her deputies.

But the adults weren't themselves, the sudden silence confirmed that. And Tublat didn't know enough about their dimension yet.

Dozens of feet shuffled below her, and she heard the front door open. Then a bunch of fireworks rang out, filling the silence with pops.

A few moments later, standing next to her door, Sammie watched as the deadbolt shifted and the door opened. Dylan stood in the hall. "Let's get out of here," he said.

"Where's Rahul?" she asked.

"Outside getting the bikes ready for our ride to the lake."

"We have to get Colin," she said, darting across the hall.

Her brother's room was not dead bolted, but the door was shut. Sammie threw the door open.

Colin sat in his bed, cowering against the corner of his room, clutching his blanket and his stuffed penguin. "Sammie!" he cried when he saw her.

"Colin!" Sammie ran to him, leaping onto the bed and

scooping him into a big hug. "Come on, buddy, we've got to get out of here."

They hopped off the bed to find Dylan facing the closet.

"We've got to get out of here," Sammie said.

"That stupid eggplant took my dad," Dylan barked.

"I know, I know," she soothed. "So let's execute the plan. Come on."

But Dylan acted as if he hadn't heard her. "I am going to get my dad back." And with that proclamation, he pulled the closet door open.

The room filled with the strange green light and the seeping green mist. Tublat floated in the midst of the shifting light, his spaghetti arms flapping in rapid motion.

"Welcome, Dylan Schumacher," the Eggplant Emperor said.

"Where is my dad?" Dylan screamed at the creature.

"Why don't you come find out."

Sammie screamed and reached for Dylan, but he got pulled into the closet like they had been pulled into the lake, in a vortex of swirling green light. Sammie shield her eyes against the brightness and when she could see again, Dylan was gone, with just Tublat floating in his empty fluorescent space.

"Colin." She reached for her brother, but he wasn't there.

"I have your little relative as well," Tublat taunted her, "a happy accident. He was standing too close to the Dylan, I guess."

"Give them back!" she roared.

"Oh, Samantha Stadler, you are in no place to bargain. And my new servants are coming to collect you."

Sammie looked to the doorway and found one of the neighbors standing there, a tall skinny man whose name she couldn't recall. Dad had helped him clear a fallen tree out of his front yard once.

"Come down to the party," the neighbor man said, his voice the same creepy monotone her parents had been using.

She looked around the room and saw the fire escape ladder under Colin's bed, but she didn't have time to use it; the neighbor would get her before she could.

Just then her dad appeared behind the tall man. "Jack? What are you doing up here?" He spoke in his normal voice. He shook his head, his expression confused.

"Go back down to the party, Randall Stadler," Jack replied in the creepy voice. Tublat shifted in the closet, his arms slowing their movement.

"You shouldn't be up here, Jack," her father said, stronger, stepping close behind him. "You need to go downstairs Jack. Actually, I need you to leave."

Jack turned to face her dad, and Sammie knew it was her chance. She ran and slammed the door behind him.

She went to the closet. "I'll be back," she hissed as she closed the closet.

She rushed to the window and threw it open. She pulled out the ladder and attached it to the window sill. Once it was secure, she tossed it down, and it thankfully held. She took a deep breath, shouting from the hallway making her nervous. Her dad was back, at least for a moment, but she couldn't be sure how long. So she climbed.

When she got halfway down, she saw a group of three or four adults come out the front door looking up at her with the forced expressions of those under Tublat's control. She recognized them as more folks from the town, including Cynthia Rudding and her purple hair.

Sammie let go of the ladder and dropped the rest of the way, tumbling down into the grass. She jumped to her feet, but the adults were nearly on her.

A flash of sound stopped them, a scream from the megaphone. All four of them reached up to their ears, their blank stares replaced by confused pain.

Rahul stood next to her, the megaphone at his feet, three bikes behind him on the driveway. Sammie scooped up the megaphone and ran for her bike.

"Where's Dylan?" Rahul climbed on his bike.

"Tublat got him." She could barely say the words, tears nearly choking them away.

"Crap."

"And Colin." She started crying then.

"Crap. Crap."

The stunned adults had regained their composure and were moving toward them like zombies across the lawn.

"Move!" she said, strapping the megaphone to her handle bars. And they sped off, leaving the adults behind.

"We will come for you," Cynthia Rudding called in Tublat's voice.

"Once this town is ours, we will come for you," another woman shouted.

Sammie did not look back but blinked the tears from her eyes and kept biking as hard as she could.

―――

After about a half mile, Sammie pulled to a stop, her heart moving faster from what had happened in the house than from biking as hard as she could. Despite her lightning pace, Rahul had kept up better than ever, stopping beside her.

"What do we do now?" he asked.

What should they do? The plan had not worked. They had gotten Sammie out of the house, but Dylan's anger had derailed their escape. And using her as bait hadn't worked. Eggplant dude knew she'd escaped, but looking at the dark street behind them, he hadn't sent anyone after them.

But she'd seen a weakness in Tublat's control.

"My dad helped me escape," Sammie managed to say

without crying, but just barely.

"Your dad? You mean he wasn't being controlled by the eggplant?"

She shook her head. "A friend of my dad's was under Tublat's control, and when Dad saw the guy coming after me, he snapped out of it."

Rahul nodded, his face serious. "So there's a weakness. His control is not total."

But so what? Even if Sammie could get her parents to snap out of it, what were they against a bunch of other adults? And Tublat had mentioned an army. What would his army look like?

"We should call Sheriff Masters," Sammie said after thinking it all over. "She said she'd help us. And I trust her."

"Trust isn't the issue."

They both jumped at a third voice, and a dark figure stepped from the tree line.

Standing in the faint light of a streetlamp was Ms. Dillwater. She wasn't dressed anything like their former teacher, but it was definitely her face. She wore sleek black clothes, almost like a combination between a spy and Batman. She had guns at each hip and her belt was filled with little devices Sammie couldn't figure out. She wasn't wearing Ms. Dillwater's big bug glasses, either. Her long, black hair was still pulled behind her head in a tight bun.

"Who are you?" Sammie asked, not relaxing.

The woman who had called herself Matilda Dillwater

smiled, a real smile, not a cruel I-hate-kids smile. "I guess you two figured out I wasn't Matilda Dillwater. You figured it out before even the adults, even before the sheriff."

"The sheriff has you figured out," Sammie retorted.

"I doubt it. Does she know what I am or just that I'm not Ms. Dillwater?"

"You're a Dimensionera," Rahul said.

The woman cocked her head at him. "How in this dimension did you learn that?"

He shrugged. "I just figured it out."

"How do you even know what a Dimensionera is?"

Sammie ignored her question. "Who are you?"

She smiled again. "My name is Maria Cortez. And I am, most definitely, a Dimensionera."

"Why aren't you trying to stop Emperor Tublat?" Sammie demanded.

Maria's smile disappeared, replaced by a confused expression. "Emperor Tal-Shah-Farneree Tublat? How do you know about that creep?"

"He lives in my brother's closet. He's taking over the town and then planning on taking over our entire dimension." Sammie felt frustration rising inside her. "Aren't you like a dimension cop or something? Aren't you supposed to know all this? Aren't you even trying to stop him?"

Maria looked off into the distance. "This is my first assignment. It was supposed to be really easy. 'Just watch and make sure no one breaks out of their prisons,' they told me. 'You won't even need a partner,' they said. What a bunch of rubbish."

Sammie looked at Maria Cortez, as if seeing her for first time. Without the glasses and older-looking clothes, she looked more like a high schooler than a teacher. And her pouty expression made her seem even younger.

"So you don't know how to stop Eggplant Emperor?" Rahul asked.

"Eggplant who?" Maria responded.

"Eggplant Emperor!" Rahul's voice rose to a shout. "The gross guy who's mind-controlled half the town and just captured our friend and her brother!"

"Tublat?" Maria looked worried. "He's mind-controlling people?"

Sammie had quickly gone from frustrated to annoyed, as had Rahul. "You don't seem to know very much. So maybe we'll call Sheriff Masters now and get some real help."

Maria stepped closer, her voice growing urgent. "No, no. I can handle this. I believe you. Will the sheriff? And I have tools that can help us stop Tublat."

"Why don't you call for back-up?" Rahul asked.

"I did," she pouted. "But they think I'm being paranoid. They think it's just Jadirel Trum weakening his prison."

"Jadirel Trum?" Rahul and Sammie asked together.

"Yeah. The guy trapped under the lake. He's the most dangerous prisoner we have in this town."

Sammie and Rahul shared a look. Cool Guy must be this Jadirel person. The most dangerous prisoner they had? He had seemed pretty harmless. Was using him to help really a good idea?

"Just how many prisoners do you have in Malsman Lake?" Sammie said, changing the subject and deciding not to mention that they'd visited her most dangerous prisoner. Rahul must have decided the same thing because he looked back at Maria without saying a word.

"Twenty-seven at last count," Maria responded.

"Does that include the eggplant guy?" Rahul asked.

Maria shook her head. "No. He's our enemy, a dangerous hombre, but he's not our prisoner."

"He conquers dimensions," Sammie said. "He said he's the master of eighty-four."

Maria laughed. "Like eighty of those dimensions are empty space. But, yeah, he's a bad dude." She shook her head. "So who's been taken by Tublat?"

"Dylan," Rahul answered, "and Colin, Sammie's little brother, and Mr. Schumacher, Dylan's dad, we think."

Maria nodded, her face serious. "Then our first mission is to get them back. Where is Tublat's portal?"

Sammie sighed; this woman did not know much about what was happening, but hopefully she would be able to stop Tublat and rescue Colin and the others.

"It's in my brothers closet. We'll fill you in on the rest as we go."

CHAPTER 19

Maria approached the house, moving across the lawn like a thief in a movie, her dark clothes making her hard to see. Sammie's house was eerily quiet. It did not look or sound like a party was going on in there. But all the cars still lined the streets, and the silhouettes of a few adults shone through the closed drapes in the front room.

Maria motioned for them, indicating she thought it was safe to move forward. They met her on the lawn and then they all moved quietly to the open garage. Maria held one of her guns in her hand.

"It's a stun weapon," she had explained to them earlier. "I'll use it on any of the adults if I have to."

Once inside the garage, they crept up the stairs and Sammie eased the door open, expecting Tublat to have a lookout there. But the small mudroom was empty except for its usual collection of winter coats, boots, and gloves; Mom hadn't put it all away in the basement yet.

Maria led the way, looking out into the kitchen, but she quickly pulled her head back.

"There are a bunch of folks in the kitchen," Maria whispered. It sounded too loud in the spooky quiet.

"I'll meet you upstairs," Rahul whispered, and without warning, he ran past them before Maria's outstretched arm could stop him.

"Come get me, mind-controlled creeps!" Rahul called from the kitchen. "Your master is stinky cabbage!"

Maria and Sammie looked around the corner. Rahul dashed in-between the stunned adults, some reacting to try and grab him, but they were all too slow. He ran in a circle through the living room, sliding around and beneath outstretched arms. He reached the back door in the kitchen, flung it open, and dashed into the backyard.

The adults came to life, orders from their master breaking through whatever trance they'd been stuck in. They quickly followed him out.

"Come on!" Maria dashed into the kitchen and Sammie followed.

They dashed through the kitchen, into the hall, and up the stairs. They only stopped when they reached Colin's bedroom. The closet door was open, casting the room in weird light and long shadows. Jack, the man who'd tried to stop Sammie earlier, stood there, next to Sammie's dad. They both had the blank stare of the mind-controlled.

But the blank stares turned to wide eyes when they saw Maria.

"The Dimensionera," Jack said.

"What are you doing here?" Sammie's dad said.

Maria didn't hesitate. She fired two blue bolts from her gun, and both men glowed blue before collapsing to the floor.

They faced the closet. Tublat wasn't floating there; it was just blank, bright, swirling green, like a fluorescent ocean.

Rahul ran into the room, joining them.

"How did you get up here?" Maria asked.

"Easy. I just ran around the house and came in the front door. I don't think eggplant is that bright, to tell you the truth. I mean, he didn't post lookouts or anything."

"He put guards in here." Sammie motioned to her dad and Jack.

Rahul's eyes went wide. "Thank goodness for the stun gun."

Maria fiddled with something on her belt. "I'm going to go into that dimension and try and find the kids and Mr. Schumacher."

"What are we supposed to do?" Sammie demanded.

Maria looked Sammie in the eyes; they were almost the

same height. "Keep an eye out." She handed the stun gun to Sammie. "I'll be back."

Sammie handed the gun to Rahul, whose eyes went wide with delight.

"I'm going with you," Sammie said.

"No way. You're just a kid."

"You're barely not a kid! And I know what's going on. Colin and Dylan will trust me."

"Dylan doesn't even like you," Rahul said to Maria.

The woman frowned. "I was an excellent teacher."

"And so humble," Rahul said.

"I'm going in," Sammie said. "You need back-up. And I can help, even if you think kids are the worst."

Maria's face softened as she took a tiny box from her belt and fixed it to Sammie's pocket. "I don't think kids are the worst. I was playing a part. All teachers hate kids."

"No they don't," Rahul said. "Most teachers become teachers because they like kids."

Maria shrugged. "I didn't grow up around here." She turned to Sammie. "This travel box will let you move in a dimension like this one. Just think where you want to go, and it will move you. Follow me and stay close."

Like that made any sense. Think where you need to go? But Maria didn't explain further, jumping into the green. Sammie took a deep breath and jumped into Colin's closet.

The jump was not what she expected. At first, she'd started to fall and her stomach had risen like she was on a roller coaster. But suddenly that feeling stopped, as did her motion. She hung there in the green expanse, looking into the never-ending color. She glanced back over her shoulder and saw Rahul standing there staring at her, his eyes as wide as double-stuffed Oreos.

Maria flew in front of her, snapping Sammie's attention back into this dimension.

Sammie tried to move, but her arms and legs just flailed without any movement. Panic and nausea welled up.

"Relax," Maria said in a voice that was too tense to make someone relax. "Just think and move."

Sammie closed her eyes, afraid she might throw up. *Think and move.*

"Where did you grow up?" Sammie asked, trying to take her mind off of whatever the heck she was doing.

"What? Oh." Maria caught on. "My parents were Dimensioneras. They're both from your dimension, but I grew up on a different world."

Sammie's eyes popped open. "A different world. Like this place?"

The woman shook her head. "Oh no. I grew up in Dimension Ten. It's a lot like Dimension One, your dimension, but it's different." She looked at her watch and then back at Sammie. "Come on; we need to go find your friends."

Maria drifted away from her, beckoning with a hand,

floating backwards. Sammie took another deep breath and thought to follow her.

And she did. Slowly she floated, moving just a little at first, and then faster and faster. She caught up and passed by Maria, a little thrill and a little panic filling her chest.

"Slow down, turbo," Maria said, smiling as she passed. "And follow me close. It's easy to get turned around in this place."

"Is there no up or down, like space?"

"No. There's a down." She pointed toward her feet. "This world is like a planet without skin. There's a core down there with a little gravity. Slowly, it would pull you toward it. But it would take like a thousand years to get there. This is a very big place."

"Is this Tublat's dimension?"

"No time for questions." Maria looked down at a little handheld device, like a smartphone but thinner. She stopped and Sammie only managed to stop herself before slamming into her.

"This way." Maria pointed a different direction.

"How can you tell? It all looks the same." The pulsing green surrounded them, changing but not in a way that gave Sammie any sense of direction. Twisting around, she couldn't see the closet anymore. She fought down a new wave of panic.

"Every dimension has its own distinct energy." Maria tapped on her little device. "Your brother and Dylan carry your dimension's energy signature with them. Eventually, it will fade, but that takes a few days, sometimes longer. Come on."

Maria flew off again, this time faster, and Sammie matched the Dimensionera's pace. She had no idea how fast they were flying, but it seemed pretty fast, her hair streaming behind her.

Sammie focused on the green space in front of them hoping to see something, but for several minutes, it did not change except for the occasional green swirl.

But then she saw something different, like the speck of an old raindrop on a car window. It grew larger and became three. And then she saw shape, the shape of three people. Her heart jumped in her chest and she stopped herself from crying out.

Floating in the green nothingness were Dylan, his dad, and little Colin. They didn't see them coming. Mr. Schumacher was facing Colin, moving his hands animatedly. Dylan also watched his father.

As the two girls drew close, she heard Mr. Schumacher telling a story.

"And then Ma and Pa Kent saw a little boy crawl from the thing that had fallen from the sky?"

"Was it an alien boy?" Colin asked excitedly.

"Indeed. It was a little alien, though he looked perfectly human."

Dylan saw them first, his eyes finding them in the green.

He tapped his dad's shoulder and pointed. "Look! It's Sammie! And...and...Ms. Dillwater?"

Maria pulled up short, but Sammie flew right to Colin.

"Sammie!" he cried. "You found me?"

"Are you ok?" She rubbed his little head.

"I was super scared. But Dylan's dad kept telling me stories. He knows a lot of stories."

Sammie looked over at Mr. Schumacher, tears in her eyes. "Thank you, Mr. Schumacher."

"Call me Matt." Dylan's dad did not look like he had the day they'd met in front of the Stadler house. His face was covered in brown and gray stubble, and his hair looked like he'd just gotten out of bed. Big bags sat below his eyes.

"We need to move, people," Maria said, fixing one of the moving devices to Mr. Schumacher. "Mr. Schumacher, you will need to carry Dylan with you. Didn't Tublat leave any guards?"

Dylan's dad shook his head. "No need. We can't move. How does this work? Propulsion?"

"Thought," she replied, again as if that made perfect sense. Mr. Schumacher's perplexed expression showed he understood as little as Sammie had.

"You think were you want to go," Sammie said, tapping her little device. "It really works."

"Why not," Dylan's dad said, shaking his head.

"I'll take the boy," Maria said, reaching for Colin.

But Sammie's brother clung to Sammie, burying his face in her shirt.

Maria pulled away. "Ok. You take him and I'll lead. Stay close. Tublat is going to know something's up, and we won't be alone for long."

Sammie looked at Dylan. His dad had figured something out, because Dylan was now holding on to Mr. Schumacher's shoulders. Dylan smiled at Sammie, and she looked away before he saw her blush.

"Hold on, buddy." She patted Colin's head again. "We're going to get you home."

Maria moved into the green and the others followed.

Colin did not lessen his grip, but Sammie didn't mind. She wouldn't let anyone take him again.

Again, they flew in what seemed like no direction, a breeze from their movement rustling their hair, but the green field did not change.

"Ms. Dillwater?" Dylan said to Sammie after a few minutes.

Sammie smiled. "Yeah. She's one of those Dimension-era..." She almost said, 'Like Cool Guy told us about,' but stopped herself.

"She's a dimension cop?" He shook his head, surprised. "I told dad about everything. He believes it all, well, because he already did, and, well, because we're stuck in a glowing green dimension."

"I should have trusted you, Sammie," Mr. Schumacher

said, his face sad. "That day at your house, I wanted to tell you about my theories. But I thought you would think I was crazy."

"How did you get in here?" she asked.

He laughed. "By being stupid. I knew something was happening, and I believed it was happening in your house. So I broke in while everyone was out, and, well, Tublat made me his guest."

"I'm sorry my dad broke into your house," Dylan said, grimacing.

"It's fine. I snuck into your basement. Now we're even."

Another speck appeared far in front, then it grew until it became Colin's familiar bedroom.

But as they grew close, the scene changed. Rahul stood on Colin's bed in the far corner, Maria's stun gun in his hands pointed past the closet. They couldn't see the whole room, but they could see a half dozen unconscious adults piled opposite Rahul.

Sammie started to slow as they approached, but Maria did not. She shot threw the closet doorway and landed on her feet like she had jumped from a moving merry-go-round. So Sammie continued through the door, but she wasn't ready for her world reasserting itself, and she and Colin tumbled onto the floor. Sammie felt better when Mr. Schumacher and Dylan ended up in a similar heap next to them.

"Daddy!" Colin untangled himself and crawled to their dad, who was still laying there on the floor.

"Status," Maria said to Rahul.

"Status? Status?" His voice sounded too high, and he bounced on the bed as he spoke. "I've stunned half the neighborhood!"

"Nice job." Maria surveyed the pile of stunned adults, seeming genuinely impressed. "We need to move. I think--"

"SAMANTHA STADLER!" Tublat's voice rang through the room like a clap of thunder. They all turned to see his eggplant body float into view in the closet door. "What have you done? You have aligned yourself with the Dimensionera, criminals, dictators, fiends! My mercy will no longer hold sway. I come for you, Samantha Stadler. I come for you!"

CHAPTER 20

"WE NEED to get out of here," Maria said, taking the stun gun from Rahul.

Sammie remembered her earlier escape. She ran to the window, and the fire escape ladder was still attached to the window frame.

"Through the window, everyone!" Sammie said.

Rahul stepped up close, looking at the window. "You certainly made eggplant brains mad. I think he's going to chase us now."

"Oh crap!" Maria called. "Everyone go! Now!"

Sammie turned to closet and jumped. Climbing out of the closet were gray-skinned creatures. Their four legs arched like a spider, but their bodies were spindly like a monkey. They had heads, rounded rectangle blocks with no eyes, mouths or anything indicating a face. Each one was about the size of a big dog, like a black lab. And dozens of them poured from Colin's closet, climbing onto the ceiling, the walls and the floor like ants escaping a smashed hill.

"My army!" Tublat declared, but Sammie couldn't see him beyond the sea of gray monsters.

Maria held both of her guns, firing flashes of blue at the gray creatures. They fell when hit, but it wasn't enough.

Mr. Schumacher scooped up Colin and started down the ladder, Sammie's brother clinging tightly to his neck. Rahul and Dylan quickly followed.

A gray creature reached Sammie as she backed onto the ladder, two of its legs reaching to clamp her. She screamed, but a blue flash struck it in its little body, and it fell limp to the floor.

"Go!" Maria roared, firing nonstop.

Sammie climbed down, but when she reached halfway, a gray spider thing climbed down after her and she lost her grip, falling backward.

Before she hit the ground, Dylan's dad caught her, setting her on her feet. "Run!" he called to the kids. He scooped up Colin and ran. Rahul and Dylan followed him down the street.

Sammie turned back to her house. Gray spider things crawled out the window, scaling the house and coming into the yard.

In a flash of blue light, all the creatures in the window fell limp to the ground. Maria dove through the window in a horizontal dive, then twisted in the air, facing the house.

She tossed something into the window. She twisted again and then landed in a somersault.

Colin's room flashed yellow, and the flow of creatures stopped. Maria stunned the ones who made it out, and then she holstered her stun guns.

"Wow," Sammie said.

"That flasher will buy us a couple minutes." Sweat covered the Dimensionera's face. "We need to get out of here." She shook her head. "So much for a sleepy first assignment."

Maria ran after the others and Sammie followed. They ran past all the other houses on their street, turning a corner before they came to a stop, Sammie's house no longer visible. Colin still hung from Mr. Schumacher. Dylan had his hands on his hips, and Rahul was bent over breathing hard.

"What were those things?" Dylan asked.

"Nakurak," Maria said, like she'd just pointed out an elephant at the zoo. "Tublat conquered their dimension years ago. Wasn't hard; they are more like monkeys than humans."

Mr. Schumacher stepped up to Maria, his eyes burning with anger. "What is going on here, Ms. Dillwater? Rahul tells me that Malsman Lake is some sort of prison for dimensional criminals."

Maria looked over at Rahul and then back at Mr. Schumacher. "Something like that."

"So you're some sort of cop or agent?" Mr. Schumacher asked.

"Yes. I'm a Dimensionera. We keep peace between the dimensions."

"Great." Mr. Schumacher set Colin down, and the boy clung to his leg. "Call in the others. Get some back-up or something."

Maria looked around, not meeting the older man's eyes. "Well, you see, that's sort of a problem."

"A problem?" Rahul said. "There are like a billion pasty spider things coming out of the Stadler's house and most of the adults in town are more mindless than teenagers."

"Yeah," Maria said, still not looking at anyone, "but I can't contact anyone. I, uh, lost my communicator a couple weeks ago. I'll need to get to Minneapolis to get help."

"Can we call someone on a regular phone?" Mr. Schumacher asked.

Maria glared right back at him. "It doesn't work like that. There's only one way to call for help, so I'll need to get a car and get--"

"Tublat took your communicator," Sammie said, remembering what he said about fooling the Dimensionera.

Maria looked at her. "That's not possible. He hadn't been out of the portal yet, or his army. He was strengthening the portal. That takes time. So he couldn't have--"

"I don't mean to ruin your discussion," Dylan said, "but

I'm guessing that more of those things and the creepy eggplant are coming. Shouldn't we keep moving?"

Maria nodded. "All of you should find a place to hide, or better, get out of town."

"My house," Rahul suggested. "My parents aren't controlled. I think with Mr. Schumacher and everyone, they'll at least believe enough for us to get out of town."

"Excellent idea," Maria said. She stepped away and looked back toward the Stadler house.

Sammie heard a sound then, like the growing buzz of a million bees.

"I'll draw them away," Maria said, pulling out her stun guns. "Go. All of you. Get out of Malsman Lake as fast as you can."

"How will you warn your people?" Mr. Schumacher asked, picking Colin back up.

She looked at her guns, checking something on them. "At this rate, every Dimensionera stationed in Dimension One, on earth, will know what's happening in a couple of hours. Go!"

The others didn't need another word, and Rahul led the way down the dark street toward his house. But Sammie stayed put next to Maria.

Rahul turned back. "Sammie, come on! We've got to go!" Mr. Schumacher, Dylan, and Colin waited as well.

Sammie waved them on. "I'm going to help Maria. I'm going to follow our plan."

Rahul seemed like he was going to object or stay, but he nodded instead. "Good luck."

Sammie turned and stood next to the Dimensionera.

"You should go too," Maria said, but her voice lacked the command she just had used.

"Tublat wants me. If I go, he'll follow them."

"Probably. You really ticked him off."

The buzzing grew as a wave of gray creatures moved down the street, climbed through the trees, and ran along the electric lines. Maria fired into the mass. Creatures fell, but there were hundreds, and she couldn't shoot fast enough.

"Follow me," Sammie urged. "I know this town better than anyone. I'll find us a way."

Sammie led them off the bigger street down a side street, pointing them toward the lake.

"Where are you taking us?" Maria asked, checking behind her.

"Just trying to get us away from them and away from Rahul's house."

"And toward the lake."

Sammie looked up at the Dimensionera. "So what? It gets us away from these crazies."

"I know I'm late to the party, but I'm not an idiot." Maria spoke normally, despite their trot. "You three had a plan to stop Tublat. What makes you think taking him toward the lake will help?"

What should she tell Maria? Cool Guy, the one the Dimensionera called Jadirel Trum, was their only hope as Sammie saw it.

"The lake is a prison, right?"

"Again, how the heck did you know that?"

"We met the Cool Guy, the one being kept under the lake."

Maria reached out and grabbed Sammie's arm, pulling her to a stop. "Wait a second. You met Jadirel Trum? How did you do that?"

"He's been watching the town. He's got some creepy green eye cloud floating around watching. He knew about Tublat, and he knew about us."

"How did you talk with him?" Maria did not let go of her firm grip on Sammie's arm.

"He sucked us down into his prison. The three of us talked with him."

The Dimensionera cursed under her breath. "I knew something was up with him. The readings on his prison cube seemed a little off, but again, they said I was being paranoid. So he can see out, and he can bring people in, but he can't get out. That's something."

Maria let go of Sammie's arm and started jogging again. Sammie matched her slower pace.

"Jadirel Trum is a liar and a con artist," the former fake teacher added. "My gosh, Sammie, he introduced himself to you by the name of Cool Guy. Who would even do that?"

Now that she thought about it, the name and his persona was a little over-the-top. And Sammie had to believe that the Dimensionera had locked him up for something.

"What did he do?" Sammie asked.

Before Maria could answer, the Dimensionera stopped again, this time halting Sammie with an out-stretched arm. The buzzing had stopped, and the street was dark and quiet.

"What's wrong?" Sammie whispered.

"It's too quiet," Maria replied. "Where did all the Nakurak go?"

"I asked them to stop making such a ruckus," answered Tublat's deep voice.

Sammie turned to see his large body, its size now evident outside of Colin's closet. The master of the eighty-four dimensions was about the size of a full-grown cow. He floated, his spaghetti limbs flailing behind him. He wore a belt around his undefined middle, black with glowing red crystals. He flew like Maria and Sammie had in the green sky dimension.

Out of the darkness, hundreds of gray shapes appeared, behind them, in front of them, and to the sides. They were surrounded by the Eggplant Emperor and his faceless army.

CHAPTER 21

"You are valiant, Samantha Stadler." Tublat floated and stopped a few feet away. "But oh so foolish. Tal-Shah-Farneree Tublat will not be stopped by a minor offspring and a useless Dimensionera."

"My friends will come," Maria said, her face pulled into a determined rage. "This is a violation of at least six treaties, Tublat, and you will not escape our justice this time."

The creature laughed, the noise filling the entire block and chilling Sammie to the core. "By the time your idiot friends realize what's happening, it will be too late. And like the cowards they are, they will concede this dimension as they have others. You are peacekeepers, not warriors, not liberators. This dimension will be mine as your kind scurry off to the insignificant places where your influence continues to hold sway."

Sammie looked over at Maria. "Is that true? If he gets too strong, will the Dimensionera be able to stop him?"

"There aren't that many of us," she said, not directly answering Sammie's question. "But Tublat is breaking inter-dimensional law, and that has consequences."

"You speak of laws and treaties I do not recognize, laws that I did not sign or agree to. You Dimensionera, with your egalitarian ideals and silly principles. That's why you lose and I win. Now, my soldiers, take these two back to the house before--"

A roaring sound interrupted Tublat's victory speech, accompanied by a growing light. Two Malsman Lake police cruisers plowed through the street, knocking aside a dozen of the gray spider things and pulling to a stop next to Sammie and Maria. Tublat floated away, disappearing between two houses.

Sheriff Masters jumped from one of the cars, her gun drawn and pointed at the ring of creatures. One of her deputies appeared from the other. His gun was also out, but his arms were shaking.

"Matilda Dillwater," the sheriff called. "Why am I not surprised to see you mixed up in all this?"

"Sorry, Sheriff," Maria said. "I had to get lost for a few days."

The sheriff came closer, turning around to survey the creatures, but they seemed content to form a tight circle around the cars and the people, not advancing. But the insect-like buzzing had started again, growing to a deaf-ening intensity.

"I really should have stayed in Chicago," the sheriff lamented.

"We rescued Mr. Schumacher," Sammie said. "He's safe with--"

"I know," Sheriff Masters interrupted. "I got a call from Rahul. He said you might be needing some help. He left out the part about the army of creepy aliens from outer space."

"They're from another dimension," Maria corrected, "not from outer space."

"An irrelevant distinction at this point." The sheriff looked at the weapons on Maria's hips. "Are those guns just for show, or do they do something? Because, judging by that sound, I think we're about to get attacked."

Maria pulled out both stun weapons. "I can help, Sher-iff, but there are too many of them. I'm a Dimensionera. It's like a dimensional cop."

"Ok, officer, how about some back-up from your other dimension-whatevers."

"I need you to get me to the lake," Sammie said. "We can stop this if you get me to the lake."

Sheriff Masters raised an eyebrow. "The lake? What on God's green earth does the lake--"

But before she could finish, the spider creatures started moving toward them, and the two police offi-cers and the Dimensionera started firing. The sound was like the Fourth of July, pop-pop-pop. Creatures started to fall, some to blue flashes of light, others to bullets Sammie could not distinguish in the darkness. After just a few moments, the creatures pulled back some but continued their buzzing, even louder than before.

"Get me to the lake, Sheriff," Sammie pleaded. "Trust me."

"Don't do it, Sheriff," Maria said. "This won't end well. The girl doesn't know what she's doing."

"This girl seems to be the only one in this town who knows what's happening," the old cop said. "And your entire life is a lie. So I'm going with the girl. Hop on in, Samantha. Let's get you to the lake." She turned to her deputy and Maria. "Give us some cover and good luck."

The deputy, the one she'd called Collins before, widened his eyes even further, and Maria cursed again.

Sammie got into the sheriff's car, this time in the front seat. Sheriff Masters then got in and closed the door. They buckled their seatbelts, and the sheriff hit the gas so hard that Sammie felt like she might get permanently fixed to the seat.

The gray spider-things came at the car, crashing into it with loud thumps. But after a few moments, they had been cast aside, and the sheriff and Sammie were clear, heading toward the lake.

Sheriff Masters checked her rearview mirror and shook

her head. "I'd ask exactly what's going on, but I'm not entirely sure I'm ready for the answer."

"A conqueror from another dimension is trying to take over our world," Sammie said. "His portal to our world is in my brother's closet."

The sheriff nodded, though her face showed more shock and disbelief than agreement. "And those creepy gray critters?"

"His invading army."

"Of course. What's at the lake?"

Again, Sammie hesitated. *We're trusting a dimensional criminal to help us catch the worst guy.*

"There's a prison there, a jail under the lake where people like Maria, uh, Ms. Dillwater, keep bad guys."

Sheriff Masters looked over at Sammie and then back to the road. "There are more bad guys?"

They drove to the lake, Sammie directing the sheriff to the spot where Sammie and her friends had encountered Cool Guy. The sheriff left her car running, the cruiser's headlights illuminating the very spot the three kids had been sucked down into the lake.

"Now what?" Sheriff Masters asked.

Sammie wasn't entirely sure. She walked to the end of the lake, her sneakers not quite touching the water. The lake was exceptionally calm, and there wasn't any green mist, at least none visible in the car's light.

Sheriff Masters stood beside her, her hand on her gun.

"You don't know exactly how to stop this conqueror dude, do you?"

"Not exactly," she admitted. "But he's controlling my parents. He wants to destroy Malsman Lake."

The sheriff put a hand on Sammie's shoulder. "You're a brave kid, Samantha Stadler. Whatever goes down, I'll be with you."

They turned and faced the lights, waiting. They didn't have to wait long.

Tublat floated out of the woods surrounded by hundreds of his gray creatures. Though Sammie wasn't sure how she knew this from a featureless alien, she was sure Tublat was smiling.

"All this effort to get me to a body of water," Tublat said, merriment in his voice. "And here I thought you were a formidable opponent, Samantha Stadler."

Sammie waited, but nothing happened. What had she expected? Cool Guy to reach out with his power and grab Tublat the moment he showed up lakeside? She eyed the calm water. No, the three of them had not been sucked down to his jail until they had their feet in the water. But how was she going to get Tublat to touch the water.

The inspiration came in a flash. In Comet of Chaos, book six in the Sideralis Academy, Andromeda had used the villain's own vanity against them; Sammie could do the same.

"I have given up fighting you," Sammie said, trying to fill

her voice with confidence she could barely feel. "I bow to your greatness, Tublat." She inclined her head slightly. She had no idea if a bow would mean anything to a creature that couldn't bend at the waist.

"You have, have you." He didn't sound convinced. "What made you change your mind?"

"Uh, well, I think it was your purpleness." She grimaced at her own phrase, knowing that wouldn't be good enough. "And it was seeing the other dimension you conquered, the Nakurak under your control, and everything. I know when I'm beat, Tublat. And I'd like to be on the winning team."

Sheriff Masters gave her a sideways glance but said nothing.

"It is good that you've come to your senses, Samantha Stadler. My soldiers will take you and your friend back to your house. We can ascertain your loyalty later."

The gray spider-things started to move in.

Sammie held up her hands. "Wait! I want to make a trade."

The creatures stopped.

"A trade?" Tublat asked. "What in my dimensions could you possibly have to trade and for what?"

"You leave Malsman Lake alone, my town, and I will give you another dimension."

Tublat laughed and the creatures buzzed quietly. "Samantha Stadler, you are not able to give what you promise."

"My friends and I found a portal to another dimension," Sammie lied. "We found it at the bottom of this, uh, body of water. The Dimensionera told me that it's not one of yours, or theirs. But there are many people for you to control."

Tublat did not responded, but he floated a few inches closer.

"I think you'll like it," Sammie continued, hoping this was working. "Everyone is a nice shade of purple, like you."

"How do I access this dimension?"

"The portal is activated by touching the water." Sammie looked back at the water, but no green mist hung there like it had the day before. Maria had called Cool Guy a conman and a trickster. Had this all been a trick? Was he sitting down in the lake bottom prison laughing as Sammie tried to convince Tublat to put one of his spaghetti limbs into the cold water?

Tublat stopped drifting toward the lake. "And how do I know this isn't some trick?" He seemed to regard her, even without a face, without eyes to look over her. "Have your friend wait by her vehicle, leaving her weapon on the shore. And you and I go to the new dimension together. If it is as you say, I will leave your town alone. But the rest of this world, the remainder of this dimension, is mine."

Sammie nodded at Sheriff Masters, whose face told her that the police officer wasn't happy about this plan. But she laid her gun on the mud and backed slowly toward her car.

"And now, you and I, Samantha Stadler," Tublat said,

"shall go see this together. And if you cross me, you will rue the day."

Sammie wasn't sure what 'rue the day' even meant, but as she stepped into the ice cold water, her sneakers and pants doing little to curb the shock to her senses, she felt sure she would rue this day.

And then a green swirl took her and she was gone.

CHAPTER 22

JUST LIKE BEFORE, it felt like a terrible free fall, but Sammie knew what to expect this time, so she didn't flail about or panic. Maybe this plan would work.

Like before, she landed in a green dome, her clothes and skin dry, facing the Cool Guy. But this time he wore a leather jacket, his dark brown hair was even higher, and a pair of Ray-Ban Wayfarers sat perched on his nose. He stood there casually, his hands in his pockets.

"What kind of dimension is this?" Tublat floated next to Sammie. She took a step away so his pulsing tentacles wouldn't touch her.

"Welcome to my humble pad, Tal-Shah-Farneree Tublat," Cool Guy said with a grin.

"Are you the master of this," Tublat's body pivoted around, "whatever this is?"

Cool Guy raised his eyebrows above his glasses three

times in quick succession. "Oh, I'm the master of my domain, Tublat. That is for sure."

"Who are you?"

Cool Guy removed his sunglasses, his pulsing green eyes flashing.

Tublat moved back a foot. "No. It cannot be."

Cool Guy smiled big again, laughing. "I told you, Tublat, to leave my pad alone. Dimension One is mine, not yours. The mice should not play while the cool cat is away."

"You betrayed me, Samantha Stadler!" Tublat floated toward Sammie, his tentacles waving menacingly. "You will rue this day!"

But Cool Guy waved his hand and Tublat's black belt flew into his hands. Tublat plopped to the ground, falling on his back, or at least backwards, since his front and back looked about the same.

"Leave the lady alone, Tublat. She outsmarted you. Not hard, granted, but she showed more spunk than any human I've ever met."

"So what now, Jadirel?" Tublat said, his fallen body pulsing disgustingly, like vibrating Jell-O. "You take my domains?"

Cool Guy laughed again. "No way, you cad. I don't want to be in charge of anything. What's the fun in that? Too much responsibility. I'll let the Dimensionera dismantle your little empire."

"But you hate the Dimensionera as much as I do!" Tublat screamed. "Why would you aid their cause?"

Cool Guy put his glasses back on, and took a bow toward Sammie. "Because I made a deal, and Cool Guy never goes back on his word." He spit into his hand and extended it to Sammie.

"Gross," she said.

"Grosser than that?" He pointed at Tublat's quivering body. "I mean, is my spit even top ten of gross things you've seen today?"

"What do want from me?" she asked without shaking his hand. "Maria, the Dimensionera, she says you're dangerous, that you're a conman and a trickster."

He pulled his hand back and ran it through his poofy hair. "Well, my reputation is still solid. I'm not a bad cat, well, yes, I am, if bad means good. You get my point. I've caused some trouble over the centuries, and the Dimensionera have long memories and about a billion regulations a guy can cross."

"What do you want from me?" she repeated.

He walked over to Tublat and rested one of his feet on his body. "One of these days, Sammie, you are going to have the power to let me out of this crib, and I want your word that you'll let me out when that time comes. If not," he looked upward, "then I'll just have to put Tublat back on the prowl."

Sammie looked up. Her town was in danger, her

parents were controlled by this quivering purple mass, and no help seemed to be coming.

"I don't think I can trust you," Sammie said.

Cool Guy's face went completely serious, all the smiles gone. "No, no, you definitely shouldn't trust me, at least not completely. But I will keep Tublat away from your dimension, as long as, when the time comes, you do me a solid. You jive?" He smiled again.

Sammie took a deep breath. "Just don't make me touch your spit hand."

He laughed. "Have fun back up top."

And with another green swirl, Sammie was thrown back to the surface.

Sheriff Masters was standing there and backed up as the green swirl placed Sammie down on the shore, safe and dry. She picked her gun and ran to Sammie's side.

"What happened?" the sheriff asked.

Sammie smiled. "The Eggplant Emperor is trapped. I think that means we're safe."

The woods surrounding the lake were clear and dark, no gray spider things in the trees or dotting the shore.

"What happened to Tublat's soldiers?" Sammie asked.

"The creepy no-faces? They split a few moments again, scurrying into the woods. Come on; let's go see if this worked."

They drove away from the lake into town and to the

Stadler house. Cars still lined the street, and Maria Cortez stood on the doorstep with the deputy.

"What happened here?" Sheriff Masters asked as she got out of her car.

"I dunno." Collins looked around nervously, like he thought another monster might pop out of the bushes. And, to be fair, that wasn't a ridiculous assumption based on the night's events. "Those...things...they just ran off a few minutes ago, and Ms. Dillwater, she said we should come here, so..." The deputy looked almost as scared of Maria as he was of the gray things.

"What did you do?" Maria asked accusingly as Sammie approached the house.

"She saved us," Sheriff Masters said.

"Maybe." Maria holstered a stun gun. "I put all the adults inside, stunned. They should wake up in a few hours."

The sheriff stepped close to Maria. "Are your dimension cop friends going to clean this up? I mean, we've got hundreds of these scaly, slimes creatures slinking around my town."

"If Tublat no longer controls them, the Nakurak are harmless. They don't even have mouths. In their dimension, they are more like cows than wolves. But yes, Sheriff Masters, my people will round them up and get them back to their dimension."

"And then you'll leave this town and take all your weird stuff with you?"

Maria looked between the sheriff and Sammie. "Oh no, that isn't going to happen. Malsman Lake has been an inter-dimensional prison since before there was a Malsman Lake. The dimensional energy here is perfect for it. No, Sheriff, the weird stuff isn't going anywhere."

Maria smiled at Sammie, and despite all the terrible things that had happened that night, Sammie smiled back.

CHAPTER 23

THE REST of the school year passed with very little weirdness. No more portals, no more invasions, and no more disappearing buildings.

As usual, Malsman Lake came up with excuses for that night. Apparently, it had all been hallucinations from some bad shrimp Sammie's parents had purchased for the party. So there had been no creepiness, just a lot of sick adults who passed out. And Sammie's parents kept apologizing for acting so weird, saying stress had gotten to them. Sammie accepted their apologies with hugs and smiles; she was just glad to have her parents back without Tublat in their heads.

One day in May, she heard her father in the other room speaking in a robotic voice, and she ran to him, worried that the Eggplant Emperor had somehow broken out of his lake prison. But he was just playing robots with Colin, and she found them laughing and wrestling on the floor.

Maybe the best thing had been her relationship with her brother. They were nearly inseparable now. He'd draw pictures of Tublat and the gray spider monkey things. As their parents praised his imagination, Colin and Sammie would wink at each other. Yes, he sometimes still annoyed her, but not as much as before, and despite his love of his own snot and mud, she let him into her room, and they played together a lot. And on nights when nightmares filled with the Eggplant Emperor and other monsters hit him, she let him crawl into her bed and fall asleep in her arms.

It took several weeks for the Dimensionera to clean up all the Nakurak. They dressed as animal control, searching for some escaped monkeys. The story made no sense, of course, but the residents of Malsman Lake accepted it, and whenever anyone saw a Nakurak in a tree or hanging from a ceiling, they would call a special number and a uniformed Dimensionera would take care of it.

"Those are weird looking monkeys," Sammie overheard Carol Olsen, who was the owner of the Norwegian Antiques Shop on Main Street, say one day in April. And that's what everyone said. Despite looking nothing like monkeys, despite the Nakurak not even having faces or hands, everyone just called them monkeys and moved on.

The stories of the bad shrimp and the escaped monkeys seemed to satisfy both Sheriff Masters and Maria Cortez. They didn't seem to like each other or trust one another, but they seemed to have a truce that included keeping the truth of that night mostly to themselves.

Despite constant comments that she should move back to Chicago, Sheriff Masters stayed and seemed even more energized than usual, like fighting an alien invasion had been just what she needed. And the sheriff seemed happy to leave all the adults in Malsman Lake as clueless as they'd always been.

Maria told Sammie and Rahul that all that residents of Malsman Lake had been affected by some of the protections the Dimensionera had put around the prison. That's why long-term residents didn't seem to mind the weird, and why outsiders like Sheriff Masters and Matt Schumacher did. But the Dimensionera agent couldn't really explain why Sammie and Rahul seemed to notice everything.

"It must be a glitch in the system," Maria had said, promising to fix it. Sammie hoped she wouldn't.

School continued that next week, and Maria returned as their teacher, playing the part of Matilda Dillwater. Rahul had assumed that Maria would be nicer, but she continued acting like a young teacher who hated kids, and she didn't spare Sammie, Rahul, or Dylan any of her wrath.

"We helped her save the world!" Rahul protested one day in April. "I mean, that should count for something, like maybe no homework for the rest of the year."

"She can't act different to us," Sammie pointed out. "That would blow her cover."

But Maria did treat them differently sometimes, winking or talking with them after class. Maria still wasn't thrilled that they had worked with Cool Guy to defeat and capture Tublat, but she seemed impressed by Sammie's bravery.

"I think Andromeda Rodriguez would be proud of you," Maria had told her a couple weeks after the invasion. Sammie was sure that was the coolest compliment she'd ever received.

The day after school ended, Sammie, Rahul, and Dylan sat on Lutheran Hill looking over the lake. Green mist hung over it, unaffected by a stiff breeze. That seemed normal now, as long as the green mist stayed on the lake and away from Colin's closet.

"My dad is moving us back to Texas," Dylan said without warning.

The other two turned to him. Sammie had expected this. They didn't have a house, and Mr. Schumacher had spent a week trapped in the green dimension. Unlike Sheriff Masters and Maria, Mr. Schumacher was not okay with the cluelessness of the Malsman Lake population. He often brought up that night, and had even talked with Sammie's dad about how all the monkeys had come out of Colin's closet. Sammie's dad had laughed and later said he thought Mr. Schumacher might be going a little crazy.

"Texans aren't like Minnesotans," her dad had explained to her, like that explained anything. Mr. Schumacher was born and had grown up in Minnesota, but had lived in Texas as an adult/

"When do you move?" Rahul asked.

"The day after tomorrow," Dylan replied. "Dad wanted to move the day after the eggplant invasion, but he let us finish the school year. He's still weird most days, talking about everything that happened. He doesn't want anything to do with Malsman Lake. He's sure something else bad is going to happen."

Sammie had been thinking the same thing. It had been unusually quiet since that night, nothing worthy of the weird list happening outside of gathering up the Nakurak. But she had the feeling that something was coming, something really big.

But she didn't want Dylan to go. She felt differently about him than she did about Rahul. Her mother had asked her one day if she had a crush on him.

"Of course not!" she had squealed. "We're just friends, Mom. Seriously. Why would you say that?"

Sammie hadn't said it to anyone, but she thought her mom might have guessed right. She'd never really had a crush on a boy. Dylan was cute, brave, and smart, and he loved the Sideralis Academy. Could she ever find a better match? And now he was moving to Texas.

"My parents are getting me a smart phone," Sammie said to break the awkward silence. "We can all text and stuff. We can keep you up to date on all the weird stuff."

Dylan smiled. "I would like that."

"Do you want to move back to Texas?" Rahul asked.

Dylan sat silent for several moments, his eyes fixed on the lake. "I've never really fit in until now. I like Texas, and the football is better, which is good. But, no, I think I'd rather live here, even with the stupid long winter."

Rahul laughed. "It is stupid long."

"Right? I mean, I feel like it ended three weeks ago and will start next month. And we're in June."

The three kids sat there for some time in silence, staring at the lake.

"Thank you for being good friends," Dylan finally said. "Maybe you can come visit Texas sometime."

"Or you could come back and visit us," Sammie offered.

He smiled, a very adult smile, one that said he liked the idea, but it was never going to happen.

Without another word, he got up, mounted his bike, and rode away. Sammie tried not to cry.

"Do you like, like Dylan?" Rahul asked.

"Shut up, Rahul."

They sat there for a long time staring at the lake. Sammie cried a little, hiding her face in her shoulder. She thought she saw some tears on Rahul's cheeks before he wiped them away.

"Mind if I join you?"

They turned to see Maria there, wearing jeans with holes in the knees and a tight t-shirt. Even with the buggy glasses, she looked a lot younger, more like Rahul's sister than his mother.

"You're not going to give us summertime homework, are you?" Rahul asked.

Maria laughed, coming over and sitting between them. "No. But I have a surprise for you: I am being moved into the sixth grade, so I will be your teacher again next year."

Rahul groaned. Sammie clapped.

"So you came all the way up here to ruin my summer?" Rahul said.

"Yes. But also to ask for your help."

Both kids turned toward her. Bright excitement replaced Rahul's deep frown.

"The other Dimensionera have all returned to their posts," Maria continued. "There are a few stubborn Nakurak deep in the woods, but we can't find them. And they have re-formed Jadirel's prison, so he shouldn't be able to spy on us from the lake."

"What about Tublat?" Sammie asked.

"They formed another prison on the other side of the lake. They were pretty sure Tublat and Jadirel might kill each other if left in the same cell too long."

Sammie remembered the tense exchange between the two weird prisoners. If they fought, her bet would have been on Jadirel, Cool Guy.

"So I'm all by myself again." Maria tucked her knees up

by her chin, making her look more like a kid than a dimension cop.

"No you're not." Sammie laid a hand on her arm. "You've got Rahul and me."

"That's what I wanted to come talk with you about. The other Dimensionera assure me that everything is fine, that the prison is secure. But my gut tells me that they're wrong. If Jadirel could figure out how to weaken his prison cube, he'll do it again. And some of the others are nearly as devious as he is. And I never did find my communicator, which means one of the prisoners might still have it."

"So you can't call for help?" Rahul asked.

She looked over at him with her best teacher-like disappointing stare. "They gave me another one, Rahul."

"So what do you need from us?" Sammie asked.

Maria hesitated for a few moments, looking at the ground, but then right at Sammie. "The Dimensionera would not approve, but I need someone to watch my back, someone to keep their eyes open for weird beyond the normal weird."

Rahul jumped to his feet. "You want to make us deputy Dimensioneras! Do I get a badge? A stun gun?"

Maria shook her head. "You're making me think this was a bad idea. You won't be deputized or anything, and no weapons."

Rahul slunk back to the ground, his deep frown returning.

"But I will share with you some of what I know, and I'll train you on what to look for. Malsman Lake is small, and all the prisoners will be watching out for me; they probably won't be watching for you."

The sadness from watching Dylan leave gave way to intense excitement. Sammie's gut also told her that Tublat's invasion wasn't going to be their last trouble in Malsman Lake.

"We will help you," Sammie said, "but I need to see your List of Mysteries. My parents destroyed all my stuff when Tublat controlled them. And I need you to tell me what kind of weird you want us to look out for."

"Deal." Maria flashed a big smile. "Meet me out by the Schumacher's old house the day after tomorrow at ten in the morning. It's time for you two to learn just how very weird Malsman Lake is."

Maria got up and left as silently as she'd come.

"We're deputy Dimensionera," Rahul said, nodding like his Joe Mauer bobblehead.

"We're deputy Dimensionera," Sammie repeated. There was no way this summer wouldn't be the best summer ever.

ACKNOWLEDGMENTS

When I was a kid, I used to have wicked nightmares, which probably comes as no surprise when you consider my ever-active imagination. In one particular dream, I found an alien invader in my sister's closet, and then tried to warn my parents who were having a party downstairs. That dream became the basis for this book.

But the real inspiration for this book is my five children. After finishing *The Empire of the Peaks* series, I wasn't sure what to write next. I have tons of ideas floating in my head, but this one, this series involving two solving mysteries in their weird town rose to the top because I have kids reading middle books like this and I thought it would be a blast to write. I was right.

I would like to thank all of my readers, which included three of my children: Lena, Clare and Jane. My wife Kathleen also read multiple drafts and helped make the book better. My other readers included Val Ackroyd, Neelu Boddipalli, Dane Brooks, Mary Killion, Matt Mangum, Denise Mcintire, Alan Seawright, Megan Seawright, Melissa van der Werf and Catherine White. And besides my own children, I had some excellent kid readers for this book: Lizzie Killion, Kelvyn Boddipalli, Dylan Boddipalli and Malory Mangum.

A book is not really created solely by the author, as others play a key role in the process. Nancy Haight was the editor on this book. The fun book cover is a combination of the illustrator skills of Caitlyn Ellis and the layout skills of Megan Hemmert.

Thank for you reading, and I hope you join me for the next book: *The Dream Queen and the Fate of Malsman Lake*.

www.ingramcontent.com/pod-product-compliance
Lightning Source LLC
Chambersburg PA
CBHW071429260626
47170CB00008B/2652